Wally —

With love and "Merry Christmas"

from

Anna. —

Dec. 25. '69. —

# STORIES FROM MY ATTIC.

BY THE AUTHOR OF

"DREAM-CHILDREN" AND "SEVEN LITTLE PEOPLE AND THEIR FRIENDS."

*WITH ILLUSTRATIONS.*

NEW YORK:
PUBLISHED BY HURD AND HOUGHTON.
Cambridge: Riverside Press.
1869.

RIVERSIDE, CAMBRIDGE:
STEREOTYPED AND PRINTED BY
H. O. HOUGHTON AND COMPANY.

## CONTENTS.

# STORIES FROM MY ATTIC.

## THE ATTIC.

In the house where I live I have chosen to take possession of the attic. Here, quite above the ordinary street sounds, I sit at my desk, or before my fire, or climb into my cushioned window-seat, where the world can get at me only by toiling up-stairs, while heavenly visitors, as they come flying down the roof, find my attic their first resting-place. Yet I am not so far off from a very pleasant world; I have only to open my door of an evening, and pretty notes of music steal up from the instrument two flights below, and I know that a few skips will take me into the family room by the centre-table and in hearing of the piano.

For all that I love my attic best, and here I have come to live, and living, to gather about me so many neighbors of thought and fancy, that I would play the part of host for a little while, and open my room to living guests. Come up into my sunny garret!

The ceiling is not high, and on the street side it slopes toward the floor, suddenly stopping, however, as if it were afraid to go any further, lest it slip off altogether. The window is bolder, for it stands at the very edge, calmly leaning on its elbows on the roof, and looking over the street and the little park, and off to the country beyond; it has its own little roof, which is on very good terms with the roof of the attic; they have a common gutter and pipe, and agree to let all their rain go into the common stock.

The attic then has but one window, but that is so large and so high that the light coming through it finds its way into every part of the little room. Within the window I have built a window-seat. Standing upright, my head is a little above the sill of the window. So I have arranged a flight of three steps, which I gravely mount as if ascending a throne, and there, at the top, is my broad window-seat, from which I can look over the roof, down into the street, or on to the little park. Beyond the park was a great manufactory. One night it took fire; from my window-seat, where it was light as day, I saw the flames rushing up. The next morning it was as if some fairy had been at work; the great building was burned to the ground; but now I saw what it had hidden — a green cemetery, and just beyond the top of a church tower that looked like a blunt pencil, or crayon, and I suppose the clouds that I see above it sometimes are the figures it traces on the sky. In another direction I can see into the hilly country, and by craning my neck out of the window I can see sails in the bay. It seems to me that I can see a good deal of the world from my window-seat.

But though there is no hour of the day when it does not afford me a bright watch-tower from which to spy out the land, I am not sure but I like best those shady hours when I curl myself up on the seat and look sometimes out on the shadows below, oftener in upon the many cornered room, and at last I draw the red curtain across the window and watch the fire-light as it plays at hide and seek about the walls, running in behind pictures and then scampering back to the black coal. If I have anything pleasant to think about, it will dance in and out of my mind to the rhythm of the flashing fire-light.

One cannot always be thus half dreaming. If he does nothing then he will have nothing to think of, and at such times I often clamber down from my perch and seat myself at my study table to read and write and study. Everything is so near by that I can almost reach my shelves from my table. The books stand in their rows waiting to be taken down, and when one goes, his neighbors immediately lean on each other and whisper about him till he comes back. And there are a few untidy, forlorn books, poor relations and meanly clad, that lead a wretched life in the dark behind the other books, poked out of sight and sometimes left for months leaning their heads against the wall. There is one old fellow, a fat dictionary in shirt sleeves, that has been in all the backyards to the very top of the bookshelves. He began life respectably; he was fat indeed, but well dressed, until a little dog one day got hold of him and ate the back of his coat entirely off. I let him stay amongst his brother dictionaries out of pity, for some time, but he looked so ashamed that finally I slid him slyly behind them, and ever since he has been living in dark corners and in the backyards of the shelves. When I want to make an inquiry of him, I hardly know where to find him, but have to search all his haunts. He looks very miserable when I bring him out.

Sometimes, as I have said, I leave the door ajar, and as I study there comes a whiff of music from the room below, and many a time I slip down and forget the old attic and my books and do not go up again till another day.

Yet I believe I never turn to go out of the door without giving a half regretful look at my fire. That, after all, is the real occupant of the room. It owns everything, and I may come and visit it. There it sits in its comfortable iron chair, and I feed it with coal, and dust about it, and sweep up around it, and sometimes sit down before it with the bellows, and gently tickle it with faint puffs of wind that make it jump and laugh with pleasure. Then it gets to burning steadily and with hearty cheer, and I take my rug and stretch myself before it, or sink into my easy chair while it tells me stories and crackles over its bright fancies. Just over it is a light mantel holding trifles; among them a bronze monk with a candle in his hand and afflicted with a painful sense of a hinge in his back. Yet he reads calmly on. I unhinge him to take out a match from under his girdle — with his head thrown alarmingly back he still reads; I shut him up with a snap, and he reads calmly on. Below the shelf is a row of plaster casts from marbles on the Temple of Apollo at Bassae. The marbles are very large; these casts are very small, but there is a prodigious amount of life going on over them — horses and men struggling together and so tangled up that I never have quite made out which is to be victorious. So there is a little touch of history on my chimney.

Best of all is it when I have drawn my chair before the fire and my little niece comes in by the doorway, like a bit of the music which sometimes steals up to me, and finds a place somewhere in the chair, and we look at the fire, and then she tells me stories, and I tell her of the time when she used to climb into the paper basket and I carried her down to sell her to grandmother.

It happens to me now that I must leave my attic for another home. I have packed my books and taken the pictures from the walls. The red carpet is rolled up, the red cushion stowed away, the desk and chairs move off in a procession down-stairs. How shall I carry away the fancies and stories and thoughts which have endeared the room to me? Some indeed have already gone out with me into society; I will gather those that seem most fitting and so go out from my little attic. Heaven send those who sit there after me as pleasant hours as I have had, and so forth we go, my little book and I.

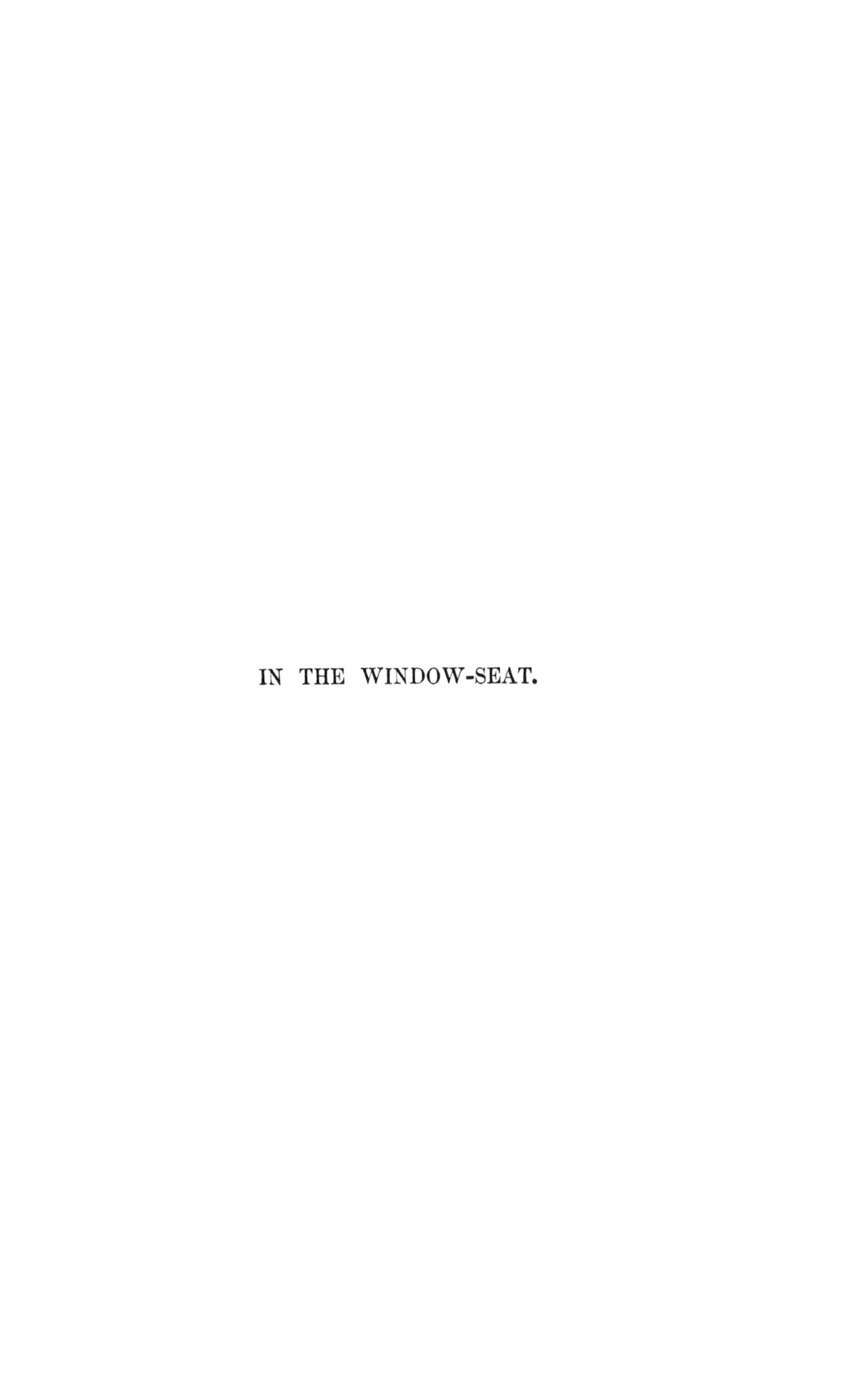

IN THE WINDOW-SEAT.

## LOOKING AT A PICTURE.

*Eight o'clock in the Evening.*

IT is snowing and blowing out-of-doors, and I have drawn the red curtain across my window, but sit in my window-seat still, with my feet drawn up on the cushion. The gas in the pipe is not lighted yet, but the gas in the coal is lighted, and flashes out of the fire-place most cheerily. It makes everything very distinct, and looking about I find nothing better to rest my eyes on than a picture which hangs over the mantel-shelf. It has no name except the one that I give it; for the artist who drew it put no name upon it, and he died forty years ago. It is "*The Entrance,*" by William Blake; and as I sit in my snuggery, the storm howling outside, this picture takes my recollections and my imaginings across the ocean, and back to the time when William Blake made it. I found it in a picture-store on the famous Strand of London, as one of the great streets running parallel with the Thames is called. It had been lying neglected there for some time, waiting for some one to come who had heard of its maker, and who would buy it for his sake as well as for its own. A little way from the picture-store is a sort of rat-hole alley-way leading from the Strand, and called Fountain Court. There are a great many such courts in London; one sees a dark passage-way not much larger than a man's body, and going in through an arch he comes out into a little court, closed all about, and occupied by dingy houses. In this dismal Fountain Court, which looked as if it had never heard of even a pail of water, was a house which I went to look at, because in it had lived once William Blake. Some old clothes were hanging out of the windows, and some slatternly women and children were about. It was no doubt a little cleaner looking when William Blake and his wife lived there, and from the window of one of these two rooms they could get a glimpse of the river and hills beyond, but it never could have been a very bright or cheerful spot. I fear that most people living there would become like the place — stupid and indifferent to anything higher or better than a pipe and a glass of beer.

Here, however, William Blake lived, and painted pictures, and wrote poems, and his pictures became more wonderful as he grew older.

He painted what he saw about him. Fountain Court, and people going through it with mugs of beer in their hands? No, for he was not looking at such sights much. When he was a little boy, he came home one day and told his mother that he had seen a tree filled with angels, bright angelic wings bespangling every bough, like stars; and again, going out into the fields, where the hay-makers were at work, he saw them raking hay, and amid them were bright angels walking. We sometimes say, especially in hymns, that with the eye of faith we may see the heavenly country and the spirits that dwell there, but our eyes are nevertheless looking hard at the ground or the bricks about us. Now Blake had this eye of faith, and so clear was it that he constantly seemed to be seeing beautiful or terrible spirits, when others saw nothing but muddy London streets, and so what he saw he painted.

There were some around him who cared for these things, but most people could not see what he saw, and they blamed him for being so foolish. He did not mind them. He said that God was showing him these wonderful sights, and it would not be right if he were to turn away and look at what other men cared about, even though he could then paint pictures which men would admire, and give him great sums of money for. Once he wrote about himself, —

> " The Angel who presided at my birth
> Said : 'Little creature, formed of joy and mirth,
> Go love without the help of anything on earth.' "

But when any listened to him, or spoke, who felt as he did, they loved him more than they could tell. They were few who cared for him and his work, but he said: " I see the face of my Heavenly Father: He lays His hand upon my head, and gives a blessing to all my work."

When he drew a face, he was thinking of what the man had suffered and enjoyed, and how much he had thought of those things which would last forever, and how little of what was soon to pass away. He drew many pictures of the life of Job. You who have read the Book of Job in the Bible know that it is wonderful and deep, and that it has not much to say about the destruction of Job's house, and the disease which wasted Job; but a great deal concerning God, and the stars which he made, and man's soul, more wonderful than the stars. So Blake, as if he had been with Job and his friends, put into pictures what they felt, and the pictures are only less glorious than the words which we can read.

Besides painting what he saw, Blake wrote down what he heard, and some very strange things he wrote, for his ear was like a musical instrument out of tune in some of its notes; when these were struck there was a discord, and we can make out no tune; but some of the notes were clear, and when these were struck, a beautiful sound went out, which Blake caught in words and sang for us. Whatever was simple and truthful and lovely went to his heart; and he was not easily deceived by outside appearances, but knew how to see a heart that could be touched, even when most would think the owner of it a hard and hateful man; if there was anything worth loving, he was quite sure to love it, because he knew that God did too. Here are some lines of his upon

THE CHIMNEY-SWEEPER.

When my mother died I was very young,
And my father sold me while yet my tongue
Could scarcely cry, "'weep, 'weep! 'weep, 'weep!"
So your chimneys I sweep, and in soot I sleep.

There's little Tom Dacre, who cried when his head,
That curled like a lamb's back, was shaved; so I said, —
"Hush, Tom! never mind it, for when your head's bare,
You know that the soot cannot spoil your white hair."

And so he was quiet, and that very night,
As Tom was a sleeping, he had such a sight:

That thousands of sweepers, Dick, Joe, Ned, and Jack,
Were all of them lock'd up in coffins of black.

And by came an angel who had a bright key,
And he opened the coffins and set them all free;
Then down a green plain, leaping, laughing, they run,
And wash in a river, and shine in the sun.

Then naked and white, all their bags left behind,
They rise upon clouds and sport in the wind;
And the angel told Tom, "If he'd be a good boy,
He'd have God for his father, and never want joy."

And so Tom awoke, and we rose in the dark,
And got, with our bags and our brushes, to work;
Though the morning was cold, Tom was happy and warm,
So, if all do their duty, they need not fear harm.

Here is another, which is called

THE LITTLE BLACK BOY.

My mother bore me in the Southern wild,
And I am black, but oh, my soul is white;
White as an angel is the English child,
But I am black, as if bereaved of light.

My mother taught me underneath a tree,
And sitting down before the heat of day,
She took me on her lap and kissèd me,
And, pointing to the East, began to say:

"Look on the rising sun, — there God does live,
And gives His light, and gives His heat away;
And flowers, and trees, and beasts, and men receive
Comfort in morning, joy in the noonday.

"And we are put on earth a little space,
  That we may learn to bear the beams of love;
And these black bodies, and this sunburnt face,
  Are but a cloud, and like a shady grove.

"For when our souls have learnt the heat to bear,
  The cloud will vanish, we shall hear His voice
Saying, 'Come out from the grove, my love and care,
  And round my golden tent like lambs rejoice.'"

Thus did my mother say, and kissèd me,
  And thus I say to little English boy:
"When I from black, and he from white cloud free,
  And round the tent of God like lambs we joy,

I'll shade him from the heat till he can bear
  To lean in joy upon our Father's knee;
And then I'll stand and stroke his silver hair,
  And be like him, and he will then love me."

Those who have "The Children's Garland," a very pleasing little collection of poetry for children, will find two of Blake's poems in it, and I will give just one more: —

THE LAMB.

  Little lamb, who made thee?
  Dost thou know who made thee,
Gave thee life, and bade thee feed
By the stream and o'er the mead;
Gave thee clothing of delight, —
Softest clothing, woolly, bright;
Gave thee such a tender voice,
Making all the vales rejoice;

Little lamb, who made thee?
Dost thou know who made thee?

Little lamb, I'll tell thee;
Little lamb, I'll tell thee:
He is callèd by thy name,
For He calls himself a Lamb:
He is meek, and He is mild,
He became a little child.
I a child, and thou a lamb,
We are callèd by His name.
Little lamb, God bless thee!
Little lamb, God bless thee!

William Blake was not always happy, even though he had such beautiful sights before him; many times he was harsh and bitter, oftener he was weighed down with troubles, but one thing he never lost sight of — that to live in the love of God was what would last; and, remembering this, he beat down whatever rose to disturb it, whether discomfort about him or sinful enemies within; so that at the last of life, when he lay down poor and almost neglected, save by his beloved wife and a very few steadfast friends, he chanted and sang melodies that rose from his heart to his lips, and with these bright songs and happy words, he left the world.

I look once more at the picture over my mantel. It is not hard to read it after reading of Blake. Two angelic beings stand waiting at the opening doors, their faces turned wistfully downward to the cloud below, out of which ascends one whose face we do not see, but whose hands are outstretched as she rises to that world which she has seen with the eye of faith. Now the doors are open for her. So, like William Blake, she enters in.

*Eleven o'clock in the Morning.*

That was in the winter time when I sat in my window-seat. It is warm enough now to sit with the window open and look out-of-doors. I look over the roofs of houses and see churches that rise higher, and from the street below comes the sound of children playing on the little square of smiling green, with its fountain of laughing water. The churches and the children, the children and the churches run in my mind, and suddenly there comes to me the recollection of a festival which I once attended on the very first day of this summer month, — a festival in a great church in the heart of a great city. St. Paul's Cathedral in London is greater than any church which any of us know in America; when one climbs the hill on which it stands, coming up through crooked lanes and crowded streets, he comes suddenly upon this great building which gathers around and beneath a lofty dome lifted high above all the houses about, higher even than the smoke that hangs over the city. It is of white stone, which has become so darkened in many places by the smoke and grime and fog of London, that one thinks of it as a black building upon which the moon is shining, and very beautifully do the long rays of white steal down into the blackness.

It was this Cathedral that I entered on the forenoon of the first day of June, while omnibuses and drays and carriages were rumbling in the streets, and all London had opened its millions of eyes and was busy with its millions of hands. Into the church I went and sat beneath the great dome. There was a sound here, too, but it was of thousands of little voices whispering, and thousands of little hands rustling. Around the dome, from floor to gallery, had been built tiers of wooden seats, and there came filing in troops of children, who climbed in order, and took their places on the benches, until there were five thousand boys and girls filling the seats.

They were children from the charity schools of London, and each school was dressed in uniform, but all the schools were not dressed alike; so that one saw green and blue and orange and white ribbons of clean little children floating down to the floor. Little girls in droll white caps, yellow sleeves, and blue dresses, with white kerchiefs, sat together above; while below were boys in dark-blue clothes and broad white collars. By each school or class was a teacher, and against one of the pillars was hung a little box, in which stood the leader of music. Below were thousands more of older people who had come to hear the children sing.

There was service held. At the time of prayer five thousand little hands rustled and covered the eyes, the girls lifting their white aprons. But at the time of singing, one pure song rose from the sweet fresh voices. I could not hear the reader; he was too far away; but every now and then, on what seemed perfect stillness, there rose from the children's throats a song of praise, or the simple *Amen*, which seemed to rise as on wings, and pass up the high dome, up through the windows, far above, escaping to heaven. Last of all came that chorus, which, perhaps, some of you have heard from great choirs, — *Hallelujah! for the Lord God omnipotent reigneth: the kingdom of this world is becôme the kingdom of our Lord and of His Christ, and He shall reign forever and ever,*

*King of kings, and Lord of lords. Hallelujah!* It was the musician Handel, the writer of the music for these words, who began this yearly celebration in the days of George the Third.

When all was over, I went and stood by the door outside. The children passed out by two and two, led by parish beadles who walked before with staves, and so they moved away down the London streets to their homes again. As I stood there I thought of one who had also seen these children and heard them sing years ago; one who sang in his heart when their voices were lifted up, and who wrote afterward what he sang to himself. It was William Blake that wrote these words: —

### HOLY THURSDAY.

'Twas on a Holy Thursday, their innocent faces clean,
Came children walking two and two, in red and blue and green;
Gray-headed beadles walked before, with wands as white as snow,
Till into the high dome of Paul's they like Thames' waters flow.

Oh what a multitude they seemed, these flowers of London town,
Seated in companies they were, with radiance all their own;
The hum of multitudes was there, but multitudes of lambs,
Thousands of boys and girls raising their innocent hands.

Now like a mighty wind they raise to heaven the voice of song,
Or like harmonious thunderings the seats of heaven among;

Beneath them sit the aged men, wise guardians of the poor:
Then cherish pity, lest you drive an angel from your door.

The children must be singing to-day. I do not see the churches; I do not hear the children playing in the street; I am under the dome of St. Paul's: a mighty Hallelujah is rising.

## HENS.

*At Cackling-time.*

It is useless for me to pretend that I see hens from my city window-seat. There is not even a weathercock in sight, but my cushioned roost is just as much a place for me to see things from with my memory's eye, as with the real ones that wander out-doors and in, like hens themselves, picking up one object and another in an aimless sort of way and cackling over them. I remember a delightful evening when I was out driving by the banks of the Charles River, in Massachusetts. We came to a spot which was hemmed in behind a hill and bounded in front by the river, while on the side was a thick wood; the place was flat grass-land, and looked like a small camp. It was, in fact, a camp of hens. Only the most venturesome ever strayed near the wood, and they had no wish to go into the river. A half dozen rude shanties stood together, and dozens of little coops lay scattered about. It was sun-down, and the hens and crowers had all gone to roost, while those that had broods were snugly housed in the coops. But the farmer obligingly went in, and routed out the sleepy fowls from their houses. It was a funny sight to see them come tumbling, cackling, and crowing out of the shanties, one after the other, each seemingly whiter than the last; for the wonder was there was not a black feather among them, and there were over two hundred old fellows and as many chickens: all were pure white, and the man had, at one time, five hundred perfectly white fowls. The whole company were clacking about as if waked out of dreams, strutting around in a bewildered manner. The farmer showered corn among them, but they did not seem to pay much attention to that. They walked sleepily about, and at last, one by one, found their way back to their roosts, where they went to sleep again; and, I have no doubt, to this day, such of them as live, talk over that time when, somehow, they had two days in one.

I have known several hens quite intimately, and some by reputation. One I have not heard of for some time, but it was living forty years ago on one leg, having lost the other by being run over, I think. It hopped about in a lively fashion, picking up a living, and seemed to be thought none the less of for being one-legged. A hen is a gentle-looking creature, and seems to be so foolish that if a carriage is coming along the road, she will scuttle across the road in front of it to get out of its way, instead of staying still where she is. But did you ever see a hen with a brood of chickens under her, — how she gathers them under her wings and will stay in the cold if she can only keep them warm, — and how she guards them so carefully that she is really fierce toward any one who tries to get her chicks away? I have seen this, and I have read, as, no doubt, some of you have, of One who loved men so, that when they would not come to Him for His blessing, He said, sadly, "How often would I have gathered thy children together, even as a hen gathereth her chickens under her wings, and ye would not!" If the Saviour can speak of the hen thus, I think we may be reminded of Him and His words by a great many things which we see constantly, — the wheat growing in the field, the doves that fly about the streets, the lambs that are on the hills, and the boat that rocks on the waves.

## A STORY THAT I MEAN TO WRITE.

*The Hour of Bells and Crackers.*

I HAVE set up a garden on the roof, outside of my window. When I was a little boy I used to see pictures in books of gardens on roofs in Germany, with little children sitting among the flower-pots; and my notion of oriental houses was of flat-roofed buildings laid out on top with flower-beds, and people walking up and down gravel walks. Now that I am grown up, I have a garden four feet long and nine — inches broad; but as the roof is rather narrow, I have to sit inside on my window-seat and admire my garden. To make sure of having flowers, I planted verbenas and heliotropes just ready to blossom, and one tuft of lobelia already in flower; so I consider my garden a very flourishing one. Besides, there are morning-glory seeds in the box, and when the vines are grown I think that they will climb over my window, and make it so dark with blue flowers and green leaves that I shall have to desert my window-seat and go into the country for light.

Just now, looking into my garden, and over it into the street, and beyond and up into the sky, I begin to think of a story which I mean to tell some day, but which just now is a little backward, like the mignonette and morning-glory seeds in my garden. I have long wanted to tell the story, and once began it and wrote a few sentences. It is to be a story about a Rocket. I have not decided yet why and where the Rocket is to be let off; but there is to be a little boy to touch it off, and I have had some thoughts of fastening something on to the Rocket which it shall carry up into the sky. Once I thought of having a grasshopper skip on to it just as it was going up, — a very ambitious and self-conceited grasshopper who would be telling his neighbors that he was going to jump very high, and sure enough, should, much to his own astonishment, jump a prodigious height by means of the Rocket. I have not thought so much about the going up of the Rocket, however, as I have of the coming down; and here I mean once for all to do justice to the much-abused Rocket-stick, which is always being laughed at and treated contemptuously, as if it were its fault and not its virtue that it should come down quietly and in the dark. The Rocket-stick in my story is to be tied on patiently and to go up calmly, without having its head turned by the great fuss going on over it, and then, coming down, I mean to have it meet with a very delightful surprise. I have not yet determined what the end shall be, but rather think I shall make it come down feet foremost, and stick into the earth of some little garden, just where a sweet-pea is coming up, there to stand firmly, while the sweet-pea twines around it and covers it with its blossoms. There is to be some more ending to it, I believe, or at any rate something is to be done to prevent the sweet-pea from going to seed, and the Rocket-stick from being pulled up. I am not sure, too, but I shall have some little creature crawl up into the empty powder-horn and make a comfortable home there. At all events, our fierce, fiery Rocket, that blazes off into the sky, is to have a quiet peaceful life in the sunshine afterward. Very likely, while I am writing this story I shall have other thoughts in my mind, and perhaps think of that cannon in the picture which has become a nest of birds; of the field of wheat that waves over the battle-field; of the men and women who are boys and girls now.

## AN AUGUST NIGHT.

*By Firelight and Starlight.*

THE windows of heaven had been opened where I took my seat a few summers ago, and on that window-seat I have sat many a time since — in recollection. I had been walking over and around the White Mountains of New Hampshire, with Grasshopper and Little Muscle. It had been raining from the beginning, and we had scarcely seen a mountain, but had trudged on, knapsack on back, drenched through much of the time, and drying ourselves the rest. At last we came to one portion of our walk which lay through a forest. It led from Waterville to the Saco River, near Abel Crawford's grave, but was only a bridle-path which had been roughly cut a few years before, and so out of use that it could scarcely be distinguished, after a few miles, from the sable-lines, as they are called, — blazes made by trappers of sable. No one at the red farm-house could tell us exactly about the path, what its course was after reaching Sawyer's River, eleven miles or so distant, or how many miles in length it was. Some said fourteen miles in all, some said sixteen, one shook his head and said nineteen, but no one really knew. All the advice we could get was a warning from two young artists who had tried the walk a few days before, and getting bewildered on sable-lines, had, as they averred, walked sixty miles; and after spending the night in the woods, had been forced to straggle back.

Then there were the inhabitants of the woods — Bears? — a few, but they were timid. Cats were the most unpleasant, — bob-cats, as they were disrespectfully called, from their bob-tails. Mr. H., an enthusiastic fisherman, told us that he gave them a wide berth when he met them in the woods; but one day, having nothing but his fishing-rod in hand, he met a bob-cat in the path, and feeling very stubborn, he sat down, remembering the taming power of the human eye, and looked the bob-cat unflinchingly in the face. The bob-cat stopped, — there were a few yards between them, — and having perhaps a similar theory, sat down on his haunches, and looked steadily at Mr. H. It was a long fifteen minutes; but the man won, and the brute slunk off.

We started at noon under bright skies,

though it had been raining in the morning, and went singing and shouting on our way. We dared the bob-cat to come out, we jeered at him, we taunted him with cowardice; and once, when we were resting, Grasshopper and I acted the scene, Grasshopper coming up to me on all-fours, and fixing a bob-cat gaze upon me as I stared at him, till he was ready to turn on his heel. So we walked along the hilly path, full of sport, when lo! just as I was calling out in my loudest voice, "*Robert! Robert! toi que j'aime*," a veritable bob-cat crossed the path. We all turned to each other and whispered emphatically, — "Bob-cat!" We listened — we heard the fellow go crunching through the forest and *meaouing* in the distance; we sat on a log, but in vain; six eyes, he reasoned, were too much for his two.

But it began to lower, then it rained, and in a few minutes our shoulders were wet through. We trudged on. We reached Sawyer's River at six o'clock, calculating that we had made thirteen miles. We held a council; should we camp here in the hut? It could not be more than five miles further, two hours of daylight were left, and we surely could get through; so off we started again, watching the path carefully, for it was from this point that it was doubtful. Sawyer's River kept crossing the path. We walked cautiously on. It came to be eight o'clock and we always seemed to be just on the point of seeing clear land ahead. We came now to a brook entering the river on our left. The path was all a maze, and reasoning sagely that the brook was going straight to Saco River, which ran by the road we were making for, we stepped into it and went knee-deep floundering down the current. We were now wet from top to toe, though it had stopped raining. A few rods of this short cut were enough, and we clambered on to the bank again, and with remarkable good fortune stumbled upon the path once more.

Then it grew darker ; we heard the roaring of water, and always thought we were coming to the Saco, and always found it to be Sawyer's. We stumbled along, Grasshopper in front, Little Muscle in the middle, and I behind. Then it was that enormous trees were found fallen across the path. Little sharp twigs stuck out from them. It must have been on these that I caught in clambering over, my knapsack banging against my sides, for one strap was broken, and tore those little patches, when Little Muscle laughed inside, and I sighed out. We stumbled on in the miry darkness. We halted for Grasshopper to feel the path ahead with his feet, when he would hollo to us, and we would go to his voice, letting him start off again on fresh discovery. Finally, not even patient hunting seemed of any avail; we appeared to be in the path, and yet at its end. We leaned against a fallen tree and took counsel together. Should we follow our compass and push through the woods? It could not be more than three quarters of a mile more, surely. We were hungry, tired, and wet. It was after ten o'clock, so we agreed to camp out on the spot.

The Grasshopper had some matches, I had some birch-bark, Little Muscle had some newspaper, and one of us had a small pocket-knife. We dropped the knife at once and could not find it again; but there were some rotten trunks of trees standing about, wet and spongy, and we broke these down, and, after patient labor, made a fire. Then we made a corduroy bed of old trunks, and propped up some logs for seats, and made some clothes-poles on which we hung our raiment, while we roasted ourselves like savages. We spent the rest of the night drying each garment by turns. The Grasshopper and Little Muscle lay down on the corduroy. I slept beautifully on a chip for a minute and a half, when the heat from the fire stole through me.

At four in the morning we were nearly ready to start. Everything was dry, especially our mouths, which could find no water. I was lying down, for I felt like it. I heard a sound above me.

"Little Muscle," said I, "what is that pattering?"

"Rain," said Little Muscle, and he took a pocket-handkerchief and spread it gently over me. The contents of our knapsacks were spread about on the ground. In three minutes we were wet through, and so were all our things. We walked five miles by the path, and then came to the road. It rained the rest of the day. We went to bed at Old Crawford's, and pushed our clothes outside the door; and in the afternoon I read the newspaper aloud, while Grasshopper mended my trousers beautifully, and Little Muscle went to sleep.

## AT CHRISTMAS TIME.

*Midnight.*

THROUGH the frosty pane, I make out the shining stars, and in the dead of night, when others are sleeping, I keep watch. When one is out-of-doors in the middle of the night he is surprised to see how differently everything looks, especially in moonlight. The buildings so high and strange, the trees muttering to each other, and bushes looking as if they were stealing out of the meadow to the road. And then at night, one looks up into the sky. There are no people, perhaps, about, to catch his eye, and his business does not keep him thinking with his eyes down, so he looks up and sees the countless stars. If he is on shipboard, he watches the mast drawing queer diagrams on the heaven, and tries to count the stars in some one patch. And here and there, over the surface of the globe, are dotted little towers, in which men sit and watch steadily with great telescopes, to see what more they can find out about those wonderful heavenly bodies. We seem at such times to be standing tiptoe on the earth, on its extreme outside, and peering up into that strange sky, which we can only ascend into with our bodies such a miserable little space.

Then there are some whose work requires them to be out-of-doors all night. The watchmen in our cities walk up and down, and see some sights that are not at all heavenly. The engine-driver of the night train peers out beyond his engine as it dashes through the darkness. He cannot look up into the sky much, he must keep on the lookout for signals ahead. How many ships are sailing over the ocean all night long, with a few men muffled up, pacing the deck, or sitting together in chat, or minding the wheel.

In countries where it is warm there is a great deal of out-door life in the night, and the flocks upon the hill-side are watched by the shepherds. They can look at the stars, and watch the meteors that flash across the sky. A stranger sight they saw once on a hill-side in Judea, when, as they kept watch of their sheep, a great light shone around, and the angel of the Lord came upon them with that wonderful annunciation, at the words of which the heavens were opened, and a multitude — no man could number them — praised

God in the hearing of these simple shepherds. Perhaps, too, at that very moment the Wise Men of the East were journeying toward the place.

The shepherds kept their flocks by night, and thirty years afterward, other shepherds watching, might have seen Him, the True Shepherd, going at midnight on the quiet hill. Did they know that He whom they saw moving along in the distance, His outline growing fainter, was going out into the cold and darkness to pray to the Father?

> "Cold mountains, and the midnight air,
> Witnessed the fervor of his prayer;"

and on the lonely mountain the Shepherd was watching his sheep.

# AT THE STUDY TABLE.

## THE SLEEPY OLD TOWN OF BRUGES.

In the ancient town of Bruges,
In the quaint old Flemish city,
As the evening shades descended,
Low and loud and sweetly blended,
Low at times and loud at times,
And changing like a poet's rhymes,
Rang the beautiful wild chimes,
From the Belfry in the market
Of the ancient town of Bruges.

. . . . . .

All else seemed asleep in Bruges,
In the quaint old Flemish city.

LONGFELLOW.

AT whatever hour of day or night one were to enter Bruges, he would be welcomed by the ringing of bells. Long before he reached the city, — unless now he were coming, as probably he would come, by the noisy railway, — he would hear the pleasant tunes sounding; and if lying in his room at the *Hotel de Flandres* he were to wake in the night, he would not have to listen long before he would hear the bells again at their work, ringing out the bright music. High up in the Belfry of Bruges, which rises so lofty above

*Les Halles* in the market-place that the great building looks like a low-roofed house, the bells are swung, and there, every fifteen minutes, day and night, they play their tunes. The music sounds so sweetly up in the pure air, that it is as a voice let down from heaven. No one can see the bells, except he climb up the tower staircase or mount the opposite houses; only the swallows know them well, flying in and out, for their nests are there. No one is ringing the bells, yet still they sound, making their glad noise above the drowsy town of Bruges.

Drowsy enough it is, looking as if here might be the palace of the Sleeping Beauty, and as if the bell was ringing day and night to wake her. Canals crossed by bridges — Bruges is *Bridge* in Flemish — are in every direction. Back of the Town Hall creeps the sluggish Dyver Canal, and it looks no lazier than the few people who walk along the shaded mall by its side. In the market-place sit a few old women knitting, and selling to a few other old women clattering about in wooden shoes; and yet, as one goes idling through the city, he sees great houses and warehouses, with quaint scroll-work on the face, and with high stepped roofs. Great churches and hospitals, with glorious paintings, stand massively by themselves, and at the street corners, in niches of the houses, stand images of the Virgin Mary and child Jesus. There is a street called "The Street of the Lace-makers." Jog down the street some summer afternoon in a rattling *vigilante* with a Flemish driver: you see the quaint houses that have settled themselves comfortably as if for a long nap, and at each door-step a knot of women and children, gossiping together over their lace-making, while the youngest brats play soberly about in the gutter. Each has a reel and cushion, and the little pins move briskly, while the tongues of the dames keep pace. Suddenly a sharp tinkling bell is heard, rung with a quick, decided air. At once women and children drop upon their knees; the *vigilante* stops, the driver uncovers his head, and gets down to kneel upon the ground, all make the sign of the cross, and pray until the little procession of priests with the Host, which was coming up the street, has passed by and gone beyond.

But the Belfry chimes easily draw us back through the silent streets and past the neglected houses to the grand square and to the Belfry itself. There is room enough here to see it, but for a good look the houses opposite, from which our picture was taken by a photographer, are best. Look now at this Belfry tower. It is only ten feet less than three hundred feet in height. Take away the buildings on either side, or rather the two wings of the tower, for such they are, and you have the tower as it stood in 1364; yet not exactly, for you must now add a lofty spire which ascended from the summit, but was finally burnt in 1741. In place of it is the low parapet which may be seen running around the top. You can see, through the open windows above, a little of the bells; below is the great clock, and below that a narrow slit of a window; this brings us to the base of the highest stage; this upper section of the tower rests on a broader one, and from the four corners of this next section rise turrets, connected with the tower above by what are called flying buttresses, or stone braces, which span the distance between the turrets and the tower. A second stage brings us to the top of the first and original tower, with its four shorter pinnacles, and so we descend to where it meets the roof of *Les Halles;* these two wings are used, one as a cloth market, the other for a meat market. Above the entrance archway is a balcony from which proclamation used to

be made, and above that is a niche containing a statue of the Virgin Mary; for, as we have seen, the people of Belgium are and always have been Roman Catholics.

A long, dark staircase leads, step by step, within the tower to its top. At last a narrow ladder leads into the chamber where the bells are hung. There is the great bell of all, and there, besides, are forty-seven other bells of different weight, ranging from twelve to nearly twelve thousand pounds, and it is on these that the chimes are rung. They have the sweetest tone of all the bells in Belgium. In our country a chime is a rare thing; and when Mr. Ayliffe rings the chimes at Trinity Church in New York on public days, the programme is published in the newspapers, and at the hour people stand about the head of Wall Street to hear with all their might, while, as far as the bells can be heard, people are listening as to something quite unusual. It is different in Belgium, and indeed in other European countries, though there they are most common. I once strayed into a little German church far back in Texas, and there saw the school-master ringing chimes upon *two* poor little bells hung above, under the roof. What a faint reminder it must have been to the homesick exiles!

It would not be possible for any one standing at the foot of the tower to ring the chimes at Bruges by pulling now upon one rope, now upon another, as he wished to ring a particular bell. To make it possible for the performer, there is a very ingenious contrivance in the chamber below that containing the bells, by which the musician sits at a great key-board, like that of a piano, the keys of which connect with the hammers that strike the bells. He strikes the keys, not with his fingers but with his fists, which are guarded by leathern coverings; and though great force is required, — sometimes being equal to two pounds' weight on each key, — musicians have acquired marvelous skill in playing on these colossal instruments; they can indeed play music in three parts, — the bass being played on pedals, and the first and second trebles with the hands.

But the chimes are sounded every fifteen minutes, and it is plain that no musician could be so constantly at work. In fact it is only occasionally, upon Sundays chiefly, that any one plays upon the bells, for generally the bells play themselves. There is a great cylinder in the chamber, from the circumference of which project pegs placed at proper intervals, according to the order in which each bell is to be struck. This is made to revolve by clock-work, and the pegs are thus brought into contact with levers operating upon the bell-hammers. The whole is a sort of gigantic musical-box, only instead of the steel comb which one there sees producing the music by vibrating after contact with the pegs, the music here is produced by a lever connected with the comb, as it were. And just as the airs in the musical-box can be changed, so those in the Belfry can be and are changed, — once a year, I think, — by altering the relation between the pegs and the hammers.

Look out now through the great open casement, and what a wonderful view stretches in every direction. The great plain is cultivated like a garden, and at this height the canals look like ditches for draining the land. There is no country in Europe so densely populated as Belgium, and every square inch of soil seems to be spaded and hoed and raked for cultivation. The line of sea can be traced on the north and northeast. South thirty miles, lies the town of Courtray; southeast is Ghent, twenty-seven miles away, and other smaller towns dot the great field. Below lies the town of Bruges; and now we are so far away from human voices and to-day's news, that, standing beside these bells, whose tongues have spoken for hundreds of years, and looking off to the sea and to the towers of Ghent, it is not hard to put our ear close to the Great Bell, and listen to the sounds that have been struck from it ever since it was first raised to its place. If we could look back over history as well as across over this plain, what should we see of deeds in which this Bell has taken a part! When was it rung? and how came this Belfry to be standing here? These great towers are not found thus in England, nor in France, nor much in Europe anywhere except here in Belgium, and in parts of Italy, in Lombardy that is, and in Venice. They are in fact witnesses in history.

Where now the Tower of Bruges stands was once a wooden belfry; but before that was built there was the busy town, with its artisans and sailors. The towns near by, like Bruges, were near the sea, and connected inland by numerous streams; hence they could raise flax upon the broad plains, weave it into cloth in their towns, and send it by ships to all parts of the world. Year by year they grew richer and more important; but those were times when there was little law quite so good as a strong arm and sharp weapon, and those who had the power kept it for their own pleasure. In the days of feudalism, the king or emperor claimed to own all beneath him,—people, and their lands, and money; he exacted soldiers to serve in his army, and money to meet his expenses; but there were great numbers of powerful and wealthy men who stood between the lowest and himself: thus, he did not command the humblest personally, but as a general gives his orders to be obeyed by a colonel, who in turn orders the captain, who passes the order down until it reaches the private soldier; so the emperor or king had about him barons and earls, almost as powerful as himself; these offered their services to him with their men, and they obtained their men from the neighborhood of their estates and castles. It was a time of war and pillage: even in peace there were bands of robbers continually prowling about. Hence, poor people sold themselves in part to those above them, and in return got a kind of protection from them. The town of Bruges, like others about it, was called the possession of the Earl of Flanders, and he called himself a subject of the King of France. But most of the townsmen did not wish to go to war under the banner of the Earl; they preferred the life of artisans and sailors, and accordingly bought from the Earl the privilege of living peaceably at home. The various towns had a common interest, and therefore they were leagued together for self-defense against marauders. By degrees they became more and more capable of taking care of themselves; they found that they could shoot the bow as well under their own leaders as if they were led by a baron. They became, too, more engrossed in making money, and grew richer and richer. The Earls of Flanders wanted money, for war-making was expensive, and they were engaged in crusading, which took a deal of money that never came back. So they went to the rich burghers, as the citizens of the towns were called, for money, and in exchange were ready to give them certain privileges, which before were supposed to belong to lords only, — as, for instance, the right to elect their own magistrates, and to manage their own local affairs. More and more these great towns came to be self-dependent. They acknowledged the supremacy of the earls, but in reality they ruled themselves. They fortified their cities, and built these belfries for watch-towers; they hung a bell in them to call the citizens together in case of danger, and by various signals to give warning or to tell news.

"And hear ye not the bells? they're ringing backward,"

cries the Earl of Flanders, in Henry Taylor's "Philip Van Artevelde."

"'Tis an alarm!"

answers the Lord of Occo.

They built also halls, *Hotels de Ville* they are called, in which the citizens met; and to have a bell and public hall were among the first privileges which a town demanded in any bargain with its lord. Thus it was that the belfry was at once a servant of the town, and a constant reminder of the power which they were holding. A citizen might well feel proud as he passed by the belfry, for it told him that he was not altogether the property of some haughty lord, but that he could with his fellows treat with that lord almost as an equal. As the towns grew stronger, they grew more self-reliant, and more proud, too, of the commonwealths which they had built up. A fire, perhaps, destroyed their watch-tower, or they tore it down, and then in place they built brick ones, adding another stage as they grew richer and freer; they were fighting now for their rights as well as paying for them, and their towns became strongly fortified cities. Their halls where they met could not be too magnificent for their wealth, nor too grand to show their pride: they were the palaces of the people, for the people were now beginning to feel that they were the rulers. When Philip the Fair, King of France, visited Bruges in 1302, his wife, Queen Jeanne of Navarre, cried with vexation, when she saw the ladies of Bruges, — "I thought I was the only queen here, and yet here are more than five hundred queens;" so splendidly did they carry themselves with their wealth and their pride.

These gigantic towers were the brawny arms which Flanders held up, as if saying, "See how mighty we are, and what our own hands have wrought!" The bell was the voice of the tower, and it spoke in all kinds of tones. In the charter of an ancient town we read: "If an outsider has a complaint against a burgher, the Schepens and Schout (*i. e.* the aldermen and mayor) must arrange it. If either party refuses submission to them, they must ring the town-bell and summon an assembly of all the burghers to compel him. Any one ringing the town-bell, except by general consent, and any one not appearing when it tolls, are liable to a fine." So we see that the bell was a very important personage in the town. Swinging up there in the tower, it kept a sort of watch over the liberties of the town, and the rights of each citizen and outsider also. At certain hours, too, it rang out to tell workmen when to begin and when to stop work. For centuries, every morning, noon, and evening, it rang for this; and such was the rush of workmen at those hours over the bridges that cross the canals, that the laws forbade the draws to be raised then to let boats through.

But it must not be supposed that all things went on smoothly, the towns becoming richer and freer constantly. There was jealousy between them, fierce rivalry of trade and blood, each town seeking to ruin its neighbor while it enriched itself. Bruges and Ghent, especially, were rivals and at last broke out into war, as we shall see. And more than this, not only were the towns incorporated, that is, possessing privileges of self-government, but, from a very early period, the various trades and arts were banded together into what were called guilds, which were formed, as the towns were, for mutual protection. To have any part in the government, one must be a member of a guild; and these societies naturally became jealous of each other's influence and power. The Earl of Flanders shrewdly took advantage of all this weakness. It was his aim to keep control over these rich towns, but he knew that if they were of one mind in the towns, and the towns were banded together against him, he would stand a poor chance of getting his money. So it was his policy to set one town against another, and one guild in the same town against another in the same town. He made friends of different parties, and hence in war he was sure of some support. The history of these towns is an interesting one, but it grows sad as we see how they lost their liberty by quarreling among themselves. It would be sadder, if we did not believe, as we do, that the towns, like those of Lombardy and Venice, were getting gains for liberty all over the world, and when they were crushed, liberty did not go down, but showed itself stronger in Holland, then broadened in England, and, passing to America, established itself so firmly that every shock felt here makes sorrowful the friends of liberty in Europe.

We have stood so long looking out of the Belfry window that there is not time to show what we have seen, but at other times we may hear what the Belfry of Bruges witnessed in those early days. It was something to have seen the men of Bruges returning from the

Battle of the Golden Spurs; and for the Belfry's sake let us hope that it did not see its great Gilt Dragon, as large as a bull, taken down by the men of Ghent eighty years afterward, — though to this day the Dragon can be seen twinkling in the distance upon the Belfry of Ghent. The town of Bruges is sleepy indeed, but it has some grand dreams. We walk again through its drowsy streets, but if we only read history well, and keep our eyes open, we may see wonderful sights and great goings on among the crowds of citizens. Let us watch for the return of the men of Bruges from the Battle of the Golden Spurs.

## THE BATTLE OF THE GOLDEN SPURS.

At the beginning of the fourteenth century, Edward I. was King of England, Philip IV., called Philip the Handsome, was King of France, and Bruges was the first commercial city of Europe. With Bruges the other great towns of Flanders had a like prosperity, and this little country with its great wealth was looked at wistfully by the hungry Philip of France. The real rulers of the country were the rich burghers who had quietly been buying the right to govern themselves of the Counts of Flanders. They still professed allegiance to the counts, and the counts leaned toward France; but the belfries and *Hotels de Ville*, which now began to stand firmly and proudly in the cities, were witnesses that the citizens held the real power and meant to keep it.

This little country, close to France and England, was connected with the former by its nominal rulers, the counts, and with the latter by its real rulers, the burghers: for it was the great market for the wool of England, and being, too, the great dêpot for the Mediterranean trade in the north, it was the Exchange of the great mercantile countries. So, whenever there was a rumble of war in Europe, Flanders looked two ways at once. Its Counts sided with France, if she was strong, or rebelled against her, if she was weak, while the wary Burghers looked more carefully to England.

Thus it happened, that at the beginning of the fourteenth century, when a great change was taking place in the life of Europe, Flanders was drawn into the struggle, and on her soil was fought a battle which had much to do with hastening the new order of things.

Philip had made a quarrel with Guy de Dampierre, Count of Flanders, and as the rich towns were discontented with Guy at the same time, the crafty Philip professed to make common cause with them, and by a trick got possession of the Count and shut him up in Paris. At the same time he sent an army to protect Flanders, which meant, to protect Flemish riches from going anywhere except into the French king's pocket. The governor appointed by Philip was his queen's uncle, Châtillon, who at once began governing the country after the fashion of those days, not for the benefit of the country but of the governor. He took from the burghers the power which they had been using of managing public affairs, and then laid a heavy tax upon the workmen of the cities. This was a very different state of things from what the towns of Flanders had been used to. We have seen how they had been, from time to time, getting wealth and real power into their own hands, and giving to their rulers, the counts, only a show of power. Matters grew worse: it was plain that the French power was using Flanders as its money sack. Heavy taxes, impositions of every kind, the insolent presence of a foreign soldiery, quickly roused the people, who had not become sluggish under long oppression, but lively from the habit of self-government. They began to meet secretly and to murmur angrily. Especially the craftsmen began to move, the rich burghers being more cautious by fear of losing their property.

The first outbreak arose from Châtillon insolently casting into prison certain deputies who had appeared in behalf of the trades to complain of non-payment for work given them by royal order. At this the people broke open the prison and set them free, a few lives being lost in the attack. The affair was brought before the French government and the answer came back to rearrest the released prisoners. But the people who had set them free were now drawn into the struggle and began organizing resistance. They were led by one of the men who had been imprisoned. He was the deacon, as the head man was called, of the guild of weavers. His name was Peter King, a man of the common rank, about sixty years old, a little, mean-looking fellow with one eye; but he was a man of courage, of readiness, and shrewdness, and a natural orator. He could not speak French, but, what was more to the purpose, he could speak Flemish, the people's tongue, and in that language he stirred them and drew them after him, in spite of the caution of the burghers.

In time of danger the Flemings had always been wont to ring their great bell, but now, since the French had possession of that, they improvised an alarm-bell. Their plans were laid; and on the 21st of March, 1302, at the moment agreed upon, the people seized on their caldrons and rang the alarm on their copper sides. All over Bruges sounded the caldron; this was the signal for the rising, and at once in every direction the French were set upon and slain. For three days the massacre continued; twelve hundred knights and two thousand foot-soldiers fell, and Châtillon had to ride for his life.

Everything now was at stake. These men of Bruges had flown at the French power. Could the popular rising become a national resistance? They marched at once to Ghent to get that city's alliance; but the wretched jealousy between the towns, and the factions in each city besides, made Ghent cold, and she would not join Bruges. A few towns took the part of Bruges, either from choice or from compulsion, Ypres, Nieuport, Berghes, Furnes and Gravelines. At the head of the forces was one of the sons of the Count of Flanders, for common wrongs had reconciled the people and Guy, and one of his grandsons.

Philip sent an army to chastise these insolent workmen, an army that held the flower of French knighthood and nobility. They marched and met the Flemings before the town of Courtrai. The battle-field was a large plain, and it seemed as if the odds were fearfully against the men of Bruges, for their enemy was cavalry, heavily clad in mail, and almost irresistible in an onset upon infantry; and the Flemings were on foot, — even the few knights that led them dismissed their horses, and bravely stood in the ranks along with the tradesmen. They were armed with pikes shod with iron; *good-day* was the name they gave to them, and a terrible welcome they proved to the French knights. Each man held his pike fixed in the ground before him, awaiting the attack. Before the battle, mass, as usual, was celebrated; that is, the communion was partaken of by these men who were expecting death; but as they could not all take it for want of time, each stooped down and raised to his lips a morsel of the turf he trod upon. Their country was sacred to them.

The French, despising their vulgar enemy, would not try the stratagems of war, although the Constable of France, their general, proposed at first to flank them. The proud knights, thinking it almost disgraceful to be fighting at all with these low tradesmen, followed their general in an impetuous charge. Headlong they rode, the hindmost pushing close upon the forward until they were mingled in confused array. And now, coming upon the sturdy ranks of the Flemings, they came also on what they had not before seen, a long canal-ditch, such as cross and recross that country in every direction. Into this ditch plunged headlong the foremost riders; after them came those behind, and the Flemings rushing forward with their "good-days" fell upon the entangled horsemen, and plied their iron-tipped staves lustily. Thirty feet wide was this ditch, and swept around in the form of a crescent, so that it held out open arms, as it were, to receive these knights. Smothered in their iron armor, a very prison-house to them when off their steeds, the mass of helpless knights were at the mercy of the weavers and smiths. They were literally beaten to death, and the victorious Flemings, gathering together their spoils, found that such havoc had been wrought amongst these nobles and knights, that seven hundred gilt spurs, the insignia of French nobility, were their trophies, and were hung up by them in the chapel of the counts in the Cathedral at Courtrai. Eighteen hundred knights and twenty-seven thousand soldiers, it is said, were lost by the French in the battle, the men of Bruges numbering twenty thousand fighting men in the ranks. Eighty years afterward, when the French defeated the Flemings in another battle, they were eager to take down these trophies of their former disgrace.

## SIR WALTER SCOTT.

WALTER SCOTT, the most celebrated story-teller of modern times, was born August 15, 1771, at Edinburgh, the capital of Scotland. When eighteen months old, he had a sickness which left him unable to use his right leg, and for a few years the chief care which his parents had for him, was directed toward preserving his health and restoring the withered limb. Accordingly, he spent his childhood, not in the city, but at his grandfather's farm, Sandy Knowe, not very far from the English boundary, and in the very heart of the country which he has made so famous by song and by story. He was a hearty, active child, and growing impatient of his forced quiet, he began to try the withered leg, to stand upon it, then to walk, and finally, to run; and so, although he was lame all his days, and carried a stout stick whenever he went out, yet he went where he wanted to; and just because there was a difficulty to overcome, he cared more, in his school-days, to outstrip his fellows in agility, than to lead them in the class, where he had no such disadvantage to contend with.

His school-days were passed, partly at Sandy Knowe, partly in Edinburgh; but his companions at first were chiefly older people on his grandfather's farm, and his lameness made him a favorite, and secured him little indulgences which, perhaps, he would have missed, if he had been entirely strong. The Scottish people love to tell stories, and down to the time of Walter's grandmother, the wild mountain country, with its ravines and passes, had been the scene of perpetual conflict between neighboring people; besides, in that rocky, stormy country, men and women had grown sturdy and self-willed, hard to persuade, and ready to cling till death to what they believed right, or loved; and the tumultuous life of the country had made people who felt alike, to hold together, and to suffer for one another, if need be. So there was an endless store of adventure and romance, deeds of daring, and acts of generous love, which every hearty Scotsman or Scotswoman could draw from, for the amusement and instruction of children. One could not take his stand anywhere in field or on hill-top, without having his eye fall on some spot which had its story, told in the homely, picturesque dialect of the people; and every one told and listened to the stories about men who had died years before, as if they themselves had been actors in the scenes.

It was in this country, and among these people, that Walter passed his childhood and boyhood, rambling everywhere, listening to every one, seeing everything, and putting all away in his great roomy memory; no, not putting away, for what we merely put away in our memory never stays there; it is what we bring out and use that we really have: and Walter soon became the story-teller of the school; and lying on the grass, or walking with a comrade afield, he would weave a web of romance, half remembered, half made up at the moment, to which the lads listened with delight. It was just so with reading. He read here and there in all sorts of books; but he liked best books of chivalry, histories that told of battles, and ballads in which horses went rushing by, and the trumpet sounded for the onset.

As he grew older, he began to buy books with the little spending money which he had, and to gather, besides, curious relics from the places which he visited. In some ruined castle there had once been great banquets, and outside, gay tournaments; he knew by heart — for his love was in it — the names of the men who rode forth from the castle-yard when all those stones had been part of the strong towers; so he would carry away with him some block or carving, and it would be to him like the miniature of a friend; when he looked at it, he could rebuild in imagination the old castle, and repeople it with its gay pageant. His own ancestors would be found there, for he seized eagerly upon every scrap of Scottish history in which a Scott had figured.

Thus the country all about became to him a living book. He read the beauty and the wildness of the landscape, and he read, too, the stories written on it by the hands of the men, who, for hundreds of years, fathers and sons, had lived their strange, adventurous lives there. But this was much like dreaming; and all this while he was going on with the hard work of a plain gentleman's son, who had his bread to earn. His father was a lawyer, and in this profession Walter was bred, though he chose a different branch from that pursued by his father. For a long time, just when he was full of his romance, and of the good-fellowship which he enjoyed with his companions in study, he worked steadily at the driest sort of labor, not relaxing until his work was done, but using his pen as a copyist as diligently as if he were engaged in the lighter task of writing a letter to his chosen friend, William Clerk. His good sense and straightforward honesty led him into habits of industry and close application, which were of inestimable value to him. They made it possible for him to accomplish a vast deal of work; and better than that, they gave him power to keep his strong imagination under control, so that he could use it, and not be run away with by it.

When twenty-six years old, he married, and lived in a simple fashion, for he had not much money, but in the constant enjoyment of the society of people like himself, young, hearty, witty, and thinking more of the inexhaustible pleasures of the mind and heart, than of those sensational pleasures which are worn out almost before they can be gone through with. He began to turn his thoughts to collecting some of the old ballads that he had so often heard, but rarely had seen in print. From this he turned to imitating the ballads, and telling in verse some of the numberless stories with which his mind was full. He obtained two salaried offices, which enabled him to live as he could not by his profession, for which he had no strong liking, and now his taste for literature became more fixed; it was evident to himself, before it was to his friends, that writing books was to be the work of his life. But now this was made clear to the satisfaction of all, by the publication of his first long poetical work, — " The Lay of the Last Minstrel." In this he reproduced the stirring scenes which had passed away from men's immediate knowledge, but which in his mind were real, living pictures; he set them before others in so lively a fashion, that every one was enchanted. It had not seemed possible that right about them, and so few generations back, such fine things had happened; and now here they were told in rhyme, which went off in the ear like the canter of a pony. The poem was a success, the greatest success which an English poet had ever up to that time enjoyed, and Scott was now a famous man, and thenceforth till the end of his life, writing books, and especially books of romance, was his chief business.

There followed in succession the poems: "Marmion," "Lady of the Lake," "Vision of Don Roderick," "Rokeby," "Lord of the

Isles;" but overshadowing these works, there began and grew the great series of romance, called still after the title of the first, "The Waverley Novels." The first one, "Waverley," grew out of the same great fund of material which had been accumulating in Scott's mind; but it was in his own eyes a more hazardous proceeding to publish it, than it had been to publish "The Lay of the Last Minstrel." There were no successful novels then existing; good poetry was more popular, and a poet stood higher in men's minds than a novelist. Partly, perhaps, for these reasons, and partly for the pleasure of overhearing himself talked of, Scott published "Waverley" without putting his name to it, and continued to publish the series of novels in the same way. For fourteen years these volumes were coming out almost as fast as the eager public could read them, — in one year three novels in ten volumes being published, — and yet Scott never acknowledged their authorship, except to the few to whom he had intrusted the secret. Of course, long before he publicly claimed them, people talked of him as the author, and he only told at length what every one knew; but there was a mystery about the publication, and something so nearly impossible in one man turning out such a prodigious amount of work, that there was a stout discussion going on all the time whether Scott really was the author. Some of his intimate friends, who were not in the secret, would not believe him the author, for they saw him constantly engaged all day long with other work, or showing his liberal hospitality: they did not see him, however, in the early morning, when he was throwing off sheet after sheet of his latest novel before the household had risen; or at night in his chamber when the household was at rest. Lockhart, who has written Scott's Life, tells us how once in Edinburgh he was dining with some young fellows, gay and thoughtless like himself, with little care except to make the present pass quickly; — but we will let him tell his story: —

"After carousing for an hour or more, I observed that a shade had come over the aspect of my friend Menzies, who happened to be placed immediately opposite to myself, and said something that intimated a fear of his being unwell. 'No!' said he. 'I shall be well enough presently, if you will only let me sit where you are, and take my chair; for there is a confounded hand in sight of me here, which has often bothered me before, and

now it won't let me fill my glass with a good will.' I rose to change places with him accordingly, and he pointed out to me this hand, which, like the writing on Belshazzar's wall, disturbed his hour of hilarity. 'Since we sat down,' he said, 'I have been watching it: it fascinates my eye; it never stops; page after page is finished, and thrown on that heap of manuscript, and still it goes on unwearied; and so it will be till candles are brought in, and God knows how long after that. It is the same every night: I can't stand a sight of it when I am not at my books.'—'Some stupid, dogged, engrossing clerk, probably,' exclaimed myself, 'or some other giddy youth in our society.'—'No, boys!' said our host; 'I well know what hand it is: 'tis Walter Scott's.' This was the hand that, in the evenings of three summer weeks, wrote the two last volumes of 'Waverley.' Would that all who that night watched it, had profited by its example of diligence as largely as William Menzies!"

As Scott's popularity rose with each successive novel, so his prosperity increased, and he set about achieving what had long been a cherished purpose—the building for himself a house in the heart of his beloved country, which should be his own, and, like the houses of his ancestors, be the gathering place of all his friends and kinsmen, where he could display a hospitality as broad as his generous nature desired; and where, too, he could realize to the full his darling ambition of living a right noble Scottish life, farming, planting trees, and making a grand Scott homestead. As with all the rest of his plans, this grew, from little beginnings and humble intentions, to vast proportions; and the result was Abbotsford, with its great castle-like house, built of spoils from all the neighboring ruins, and filled with curious ancient relics, which the enthusiastic antiquary gathered and received from every quarter. Here his friends came, and about him here his family grew; while the farm itself, under his artist eye, developed into a lovely and varied estate.

Did not this seem to be a sunny life? and yet there was to come a storm; and after the storm, men were to see this stalwart, oaken character still erect, though beaten upon sorely.

Early in his literary career, indeed before he was fairly a writer, Scott had interested himself in an old school friend, James Ballantyne, who was a printer at Kelso. He induced him to come to Edinburgh, and used his influence to obtain work for him; by degrees, as his own schemes of authorship took shape, he joined his fortunes with those of his friend, and was in effect a partner of his in a great and growing business. Scott wrote the books which Ballantyne printed, and his mighty industry kept the presses filled. Was it strange that Scott should have been thought by his partner, and should have thought himself, to have an inexhaustible capital in his brain, when he had only to write a novel, and thousands of pounds flowed in at once? But over confidence, bad management, and troublesome times, brought a crisis. The printing and publishing houses in which he was interested, failed, and Scott became suddenly a poor man — but still with that California head of his.

And now came the turn in Sir Walter's life, which, with all its sadness, led to his noblest honor. The law gave him the chance to escape the obligation laid upon him by the failure of Ballantyne, but he refused to accept it. Friends, even strangers, came forward with magnificent offers of money, but he put them aside, took up his pen, and deliberately set about discharging debts which his sense of honor forbade him to disregard. He was to roll off a load of five hundred thousand dollars. Look at this man! nearly sixty years of age, "lonely, aged, deprived of my family — all but poor Anne," as he writes, when fast following his losses, comes the death of his wife; so lonely, that for companionship he talks to his daily "Diary," yet working on and on, steadily giving himself to his task, and shrinking from no labor that may bring him nearer to the goal of his desires; warned by a paralytic stroke, yet again taking his heavy pen, which once raced lightly over the paper, — we turn away, and will not look at the failing strength, the broken body, the worn mind. He died the 21st of September, 1832, having, with almost superhuman strength, discharged half of his obligations. His family and friends took up the sacred debt, and discharged the remainder. The world will never cease owing a debt of gratitude to one who has cheered it with so many pure and noble tales, and given it, besides, his own hearty, whole-souled, manly life.

## THE SINGING OF THE SEIRENS.

### AS TOLD BY ODYSSEUS.

[Odysseus and his shipmates, returning from the shores where they had called up the shadowy ghosts, once more feasted on Kirke's island, and rested before they should take up again their wanderings. Odysseus told Kirke what they had passed through, and whither they now were to go she in turn revealed to him.]

KIRKE *speaks.* — "So, all these labors have come to an end; — now hear what I shall tell thee: it is God himself shall show it. To the Seirens thou first wilt come, that bewitch men, when any one draws nigh; when he, unwitting, nears them and hears the sound of their singing, to him no wife nor children dear stand at the door to welcome him to his home again, no, but the Seirens enchant him with their silvery melody as they sit on the meadow sward. But — around them is a huge heap of bones with shrivelling flesh, the bones, the flesh of rotting men. Row past! row past their isle and stuff thy fellows' ears with honeyed wax that none may hear. Thus with the rest, but be it thine to hear if thou wilt, bidding the men bind thee hand and foot, erect upon the mast-frame, with the ropes tightly gathered about the mast. So thou mayst take thy fill of joy in listening to the Seirens. But if thou implorest thy comrades, yea bidst them set thee free, then let them fetter thee with still other bands."

. . . . . . . .

Such were her words: then straight the Light of Day rose in the East and sat on her throne of gold. Back over her island home went heavenly Kirke, and I to my ship again, where I bade the fellows climb once more the ship's side and cast loose the hawsers. Up they clomb and took their places on the rowers' benches; stroke on stroke their oars dipped in the frothy sea, but again came a fore wind, bellying the sails and making the ship's prow cut the waves with its deep-blue blade; brave messmate that, for our voyage, sent by Kirke, strange goddess with her waving tresses and her human voice! So, straight, all left the oars and sat on deck, each hammering at his armor, whilst the wind and the helmsman kept the ship on her course. Then I opened my lips, and out of my heavy heart spoke to the fellows: —

"Friends all! for it were not well that one,

or two at most, should know the fateful tales which Kirke told to me. I will retell them that all may know and die, if die we must, or know them to escape, and flee a fated death. First then, she warns us shun the voice of the heavenly-throated Seirens, and the flowery mead whereon they rest. Me only would she have to hear their song. But tie me with stubborn ties that I may stay fast bound, erect upon the mast-frame, with the ropes knotted to the mast. And should I beg, nay, command you to loose me, do you only press me tight to the mast with more bands still."

Each of Kirke's tales I told in turn; while I was yet speaking, our good ship, flying forward, was at the Seirens' isle, for the favoring breeze drove her on. Then all at once the wind dropped; there was a dead calm; a spirit hushed the waves in slumber. The men arose, furled the ship's sails and laid them by in the hold, then sat on the rowers' benches and turned up the foaming water with their smooth oars. For me, I took a great cake of wax and, cutting it into bits with a sharp knife, kneaded the pieces with my sturdy hands. Quickly the wax melted, for it yielded to the mighty force of the Sun-god, Hyperion's kingly son. One by one I smeared the ears of all my comrades, who gathered around and bound me hand and foot, erect upon the mast-frame, with the ropes well knotted to the mast. Again they sat and beat the frothy sea with their oars. And when we were as far off from the island as a man could be heard if he shouted, while rowing lightly, the sea-swift ship pressed near and escaped not the charmers who lifted up their clear warblings.

"Hither ho! draw near, Odysseus, worthy of a world of praise, the glory of the Achæan name; stay thy ship to hear our voice. For never sailed one by in his dark ship and stopped to hear the celestial songs flowing from our lips, but went he on his way, merry at heart and wise in soul. We know all that befell thee on the broad plain of Troy — all that the Argive host and Trojans suffered at the hest of the gods. Yea, we know whatsoever cometh to life in all the springing earth."

These were the words borne on their heavenly voice. My heart was moved. I yearned to listen, and I commanded the men to set me free, frowning at them with my eyebrows. But they only bent low at their oars and rowed on; while Perimedes and Eurylochus arose and tied me with more cords and jammed me to the mast. Then, when we had rowed by these charmers, and could no longer hear the words of the Seirens nor the melody of their voices, my trusty comrades drew out the wax with which I had estopped their ears and loosed me from my fetters.

## FRANCIS HUBER.

THERE is an old familiar story called "Eyes and no Eyes," which tells how two boys, who had each a good pair of eyes, took the same walk in the country, but came back, one with nothing to tell because he had not used his eyes; the other with his head full of remarkable sights which he had seen. When Spring comes, and there is a general waking up of Nature, eyes have a wonderful deal to look at; do they see half as much as a blind man once saw who literally had no eyes, and yet has written the most minute and accurate account of the habits of that little creature, the bee?

Francis Huber was born with a good pair of eyes, in Geneva, Switzerland, July 2, 1750. His parents were well-known citizens, who gave him a good education, and he cared so much for study and reading, that he very unwisely bartered his eyes for knowledge; for late at night he worked in his room over a dim candle, and when that went out, by the light

of the moon, carrying further the studies of the day, and reading romances. He did not take very good care of himself, it is to be feared; for his health, and with it his sight, began to give way when he was about fifteen. It looked as if he were about to become blind, and his father took him to Paris to consult a famous oculist. This physician sent him into the country, away from books and college friends; to lead the life of a peasant upon a farm. He lived with the plain people about him, following the plough all day, and sleeping all night, instead of wasting candles and moonlight. His health returned, and he went back to Geneva, in love with the country, and with his head full of many things that he had noticed as he worked in the fields.

But his eyes grew dimmer, and it became certain that he must be soon totally blind. Before they closed, however, he had seen the face of a young girl, Marie Lullin, whom he was to see but a short time longer, but who was to live faithfully with him for forty years. Her father was very angry that a young man about to be totally blind should offer to marry his daughter, who had two eyes, and was to have a large fortune, and refused his consent to the marriage. Huber, in despair, used all the remaining light in his eyes to get such a vivid knowledge of things about him as should last him when he could no longer see. He looked at everything closely, and putting together what he saw with what he remembered, and what he imagined he saw, he was able to present such a picture to himself as sometimes even deceived him into believing that he saw every particle of it, just as we think we recollect a good many things that happened to us when children, because they have been told us over and over. At any rate, he used his knowledge and sight so discreetly, that it was very hard for other people to suppose him nearly blind; and this was exactly what he wished, for it was his probable helplessness which made Marie's father refuse him his daughter. But Lullin was not won over by this course, and steadily kept to his refusal. Marie, however, remained faithful; and when, seven years after, at twenty-five, the law allowed her freedom, she married Huber, and thenceforth was inseparable from him, reading to him, writing for him, and, most of all, observing for him.

For this was the wonderful fact about Huber, that having no eyes, he used the eyes of those about him in such a way, that he was able to make discoveries which astonished the scientific world, and have never been proved false. He had his wife, he had also a sagacious and devoted servant, named Francis Burnens, and finally his son Pierre grew up to observe for him, and to become himself famous for his study of ants. Huber's life in the country had made him fond of Natural History, and his interest had been increased by reading; moreover, he had a neighbor named Charles Bonnet, who had some reputation as a scientific man, and came to talk with him.

In his darkness, therefore, for he had now become totally blind, he began to remember certain facts about bees, which he had noticed, and wished to explain them. For this it was necessary to watch them, and he set Francis Burnens to work, telling him what to look at and to look for. He asked him questions in such a way that the quick-witted servant learned what to notice, and daily reported his observations. Huber's mind became intensely occupied with this subject. He asked his wife and his neighbors what they saw, and if they saw thus and thus. In this way he was getting the observations of a number of people, who all saw independently of each other; and Huber once said, smiling, to a brother naturalist, "I am much more certain of what I state than you are; for you publish what your own eyes only have seen, while I take the mean among many witnesses."

In his darkness, Huber's mind took hold of the facts presented to it, and turned them about, put them together, made one explain another; and, in a word, constructed whole facts out of the bits and fragments which different people brought to him. "He discovered," for instance, says one of his friends, "that the nuptials, so mysterious and so remarkably fruitful, of the queen bee, the only mother of the tribe, never take place in the hive, but always in the open air, and at such an elevation as to escape ordinary observation, — but not the intelligence of a blind man, aided by a peasant. He confirmed, by multiplied observations, the discovery of Schirach, until then disputed, that bees can transform, at pleasure, the eggs of working bees into queens by appropriate food. He described with much care the combats of queen bees with each other, the massacre of drones, and all the singular occurrences which take place in a hive when a strange queen is introduced as a substitute for the natural queen. He showed the influence which the dimensions of the cells exert upon the shape of the insects which proceed from them; he related the manner by which the larvæ spin the silk of their cocoons; he studied the origin of swarms, and was the first who gave a rational and accurate history of those flying colonies." This, and very much more, is recited as the discovery of Huber.

Now who saw all this, Francis Burnens or Francis Huber? Bees had been seen by peasants ever since the world began, and yet Huber, who had no eyes, was the first really to see them. Burnens was indefatigable in following his master's directions, but he could not put his facts together as Huber did. Just so our eyes may rest upon everything about us, but behind the eye is the mind, that sits like Huber all alone, and directs the eye what to look at and report to it; and it is just as the mind directs and the eye obeys, that we find out things, — *discover,* — that is, take off the cover and see what is underneath. That habit which Huber formed when he was growing blind, of putting together what he heard and what he remembered and also saw very imperfectly, was a capital preparation for his scientific studies afterwards, and made it more possible for him to put Burnens' facts into just their right places. Burnens brought him this and that, and Huber put this and that together.

Every one who knew him said that he was a happy man, and no wonder, for his mind was busy all the while about things worth knowing; and instead of complaining bitterly and idly that he had no eyes, he thanked God that he had a mind, and could make very good use of other people's eyes. He died in 1831, eighty-one years of age.

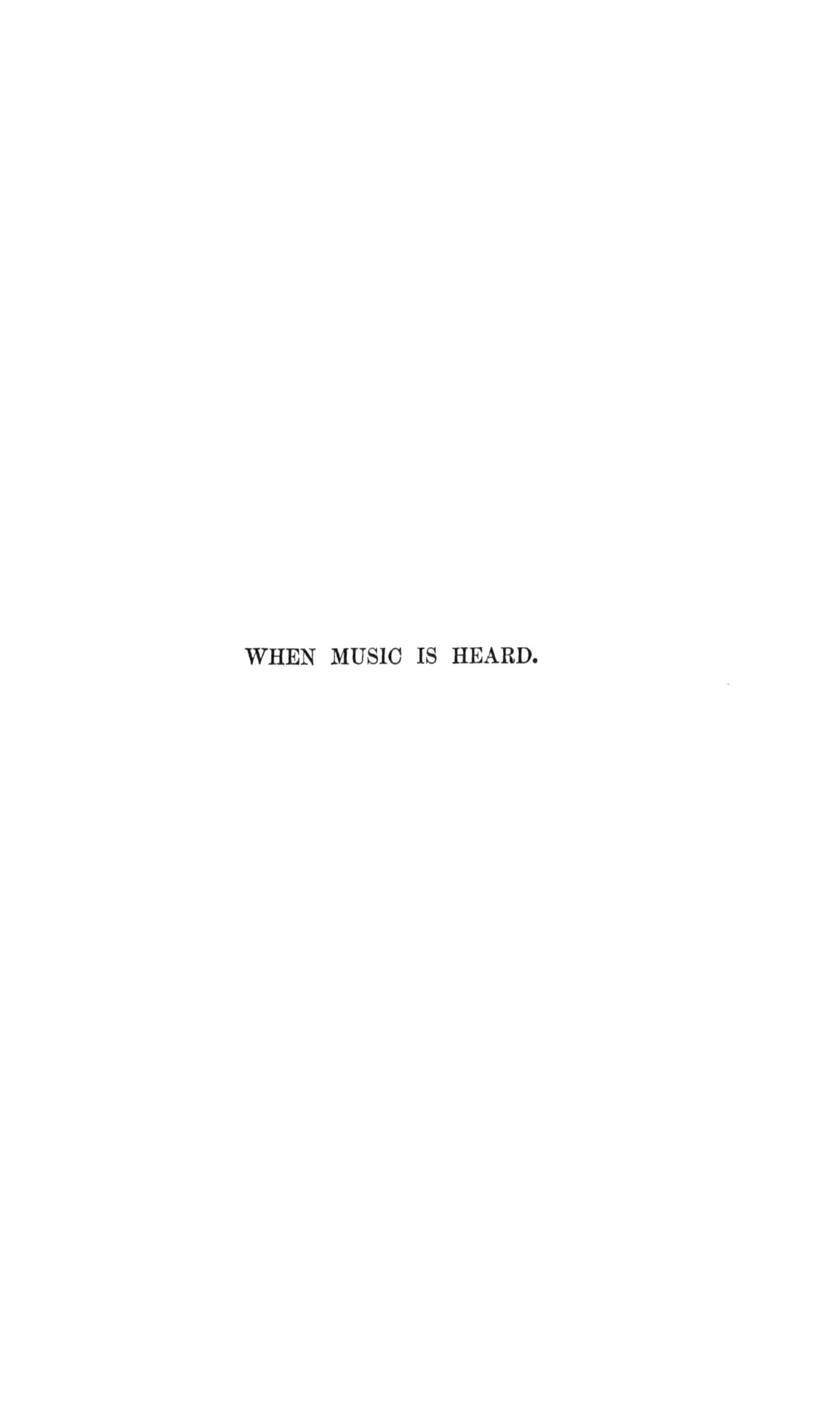

WHEN MUSIC IS HEARD.

## THE MUSIC PARTY.

There had been a music-party at the house of the Professor. The instruments were a piano, two violins, and a violoncello; the music was chiefly from Beethoven and Mozart. There was, however, one piece from Haydn which was the most entertaining of all, for in that the company also acted as performers. It was his Children Symphony, in giving which an orchestra is required, beside the violins and violoncello, of a night-owl, cuckoo, quail, rattle, whistle, bells, penny trumpet, and drum. Each of these instruments has its appointed part, and a good interpreter of the music fancies a sleighing party or hunt, a mimic battle or a spring scene in which the cuckoo with "ominous note" has it all its own way, with no indignant poet to put it to flight. This piece had been performed with great success, spite of the sheepiness of the young gentleman who played the penny trumpet, and considering also the defective playing upon the whistle. But every orchestra has its faults, though few maintain such good feeling as did the amateur one upon the evening mentioned. The parts had been distributed without much regard to the character of the performers, and the student, who was particularly unmartial, and somewhat melancholy indeed, was the one who played the trumpet so badly; the rattle was given to a young lady who spent the rest of the evening in looking over an album of photographs upon the table, and the night-owl fell to the liveliest person in the room. But just this incongruity made more fun. The company was small and well-chosen; there was unconstrained enjoyment; the music was carefully selected and admirably played; the Children Symphony was novel and well carried out, and all agreed that the evening, now at an end, was one of the pleasantest they had ever spent. The host and his amiable wife followed the company to the door, and at last all were gone.

The student, however, remained a little longer, as he was a privileged person, and it was well understood between him and the Professor's daughters that there was an entire mould of ice-cream left, which could not possibly keep and which it was a pity to throw away. This after-play lasted a while and ended with the student's asking to hear once more upon the piano an air which had lodged in his head during the evening. The piano was reopened, the air played, and the student rose to go. He noticed the stringed instruments in their cases placed in the corner of the room, and learned that the gentlemen who played them had asked permission to leave them till the morning; the instruments were valuable ones and the cases were opened for him to see. Thus it chanced that the piano, the violins, and the violoncello were all again uncovered, and what is more important to us, — for otherwise our account would have been through by this time, — they were left so, although it was very careless on the part of all concerned.

The student shut the door of the house behind him and stood upon the step outside, buttoning his great-coat about him. The moon was touching the fringe of heavy clouds and just setting out over the blue sea of sky. He stopped as he was closing the upper buttonhole of his coat and looked up at the witching sight. The passage, which had been repeated to him just now lingered in his brain, and he remembered its connection in the music. It had come out clear and lovely from a dark mass of sound, flowing along with liquid melody. It was like the moon above him, and as he recalled other effects in the same piece, it seemed to him as if there were nothing in creation so wonderful as sound.

"How subtle it is!" said he. "It steals so into the brain and holds such power over one. There surely is nothing so penetrating and which yet can swell to such compass. Sound, methinks, must have a life of its own — a personality; it is so human, it must have its sympathy and antipathy like mortals. What exquisite sensibility, then, it must possess, finer far than that of the most sensuous poet. It must have a most tremulous, airy susceptibility. It is without doubt the most delicate essence of soul. In such a guise one might discover the secrets of soul-life. O that I might for once be a sound!"

Now the reason why we do not always get what we wish for is, that we do not wish so hard as to believe that we have it; this was not the case with the student. He had become so entirely absorbed in the contemplation of the delightful nature of sound, as he stood thus watching the moon, that when he suddenly and fervently uttered this wish, he had his wish granted. No sooner had he spoken the word than he was conscious of a remarkable change. His soul, so to speak, undressed itself, casting off the body, and he would have been in a very destitute condition if the change had stopped here, since it is not expedient here to be without a body, even in travelling, as some do contrariwise affirm; but at the same time the sound which had lingered in his brain began to swell. It penetrated his soul like moisture, until he was, as it were, absorbed in the sound; but that did not prevent him from using his faculties so far as they could be used when the senses were gone, — with this addition, however, that he was now like a well tuned music-box playing an air with nobody to listen to it.

Sound easily moves, as we all know; it is very much governed by attraction also, and accordingly the student, leaving his body upright upon the door-step, was drawn involuntarily through the key-hole of the outer door, and thus by the hall back into the room where the music had been given; for there were other sounds possessing attractive power. Indeed, when the student-sound entered the room, a great number of notes, some from the violins, some from the violoncello, and some from the piano, were hovering about; they were of every variety of character, and when they came from the music-writer's brain and found life through the medium of his instrument, they were like a great multitude of people, each with a separate temperament. But the student was only dimly conscious of their presence, since he also was a sound, and like them had existence without sense. He differed from them in this, however, that in him sound was associated with soul; if he could only find some sort of a body now suitable to his state, he would have excellent advantages.

It seems strange that when the student was so entirely musical as at this moment, he should bethink himself of a large picture which hung upon the wall, and which was more interesting as a historical picture than as a work of art. It was the Death-bed of Calvin and contained many figures. Of this picture the student thought, just at the moment when he was most embarrassed by the absence of his body which he had left upon the door-step. An odd fancy crossed his mind. "How would one of the figures in the picture answer as a substitute for my body?" When a soul that is so refined as to be for the greater part a sound, has any wish, it does not need to express it earnestly; the mere suggestion is enough, and thus instantly the student had the satisfaction of taking possession of the body, such as it was, of one of the figures in the picture.

"I must confess," said he, naturally fastidious and rendered more so by his musical nature, "that this is not the most fitting abode for me; my face is not very beautiful, neither is my dress, especially this ruffled collar, nor is it pleasant to be so near a sick-bed. I will get a little farther off;" and he moved into the person at the end of the room — the syndic, so proud of his handsome leg. He proceeded to make the most of his situation. Naturally he tried the ears first of his new body, and though they were quite disproportionate to his delicate organization, they were of some use; just as a fine musician may draw sweet sounds from a wretched instrument. His eyes were next attended to; here he had the misfortune to be obliged to look through the glazing of the picture; thus it was like always being upon the outside of a window; but, that too, was only a partial hindrance. His nose he found to be quite stopped up with dust, but he was not sorry for it when he remembered that he was in a sick-room. His eyes and ears were, in fact, all that he was particular about, especially as he considered that he only meant his abode in that body to be a temporary one.

He was now quite comfortably settled, and began to take a lively interest in what he saw and heard about him. The sounds which before he had known to be present by a sort of attraction to them, he now was able to distinguish. There were two kinds. One was that of sounds which had entered the mind of some one of those present in the evening and had served as the material for some creation. They had entered by the ear and found personality, and indeed, individuality, and having once entered a human soul, were, like our hero, incapable of enjoyment from sources outside of themselves, unless harbored in some form approaching at least the human; for they are no longer pure sounds, but by their abode in man, have acquired something of the character of his soul, and hence require a bodily complement. It is the aspiration of all such, driven out of the mind where they had been first welcomed, to return again to their old haunts; nor do they obtain rest until they achieve their purpose. Perhaps for months or even years they wander desolately about, separated each from the *dimidium animæ suæ*, yet do they sometimes receive a fresh welcome; what wonder then, that readmitted, they persistently remain, and all day long we work and play and read to the melody which will not away from our minds? These, therefore, had, like our hero, obtained various tenements: one, more fortunate than the rest, in the face and chest of the lovable Mozart; one in the faces that make up the Sistine Madonna; out of the eyes of the two cherubs looked forth others, and the cloud-faces swarmed with them. Some had established themselves in the various personages in the large picture already mentioned. Even the Professor's grandfather's portrait in oil was not without its lodger; and the image of the lively Zouave that stood upon a bracket, surmounted by a feather, housed a very merry sound.

But these were not the only ones. Our student, in his sound-soul, did gain something from his bereft condition, for he was able to see what would have been forbidden to his merely physical eyes. There were a multitude of sounds present which belonged to no one but themselves, and which never had been inclosed in a human soul; these were such as had, to use a familiar expression, entered one ear and passed out of the other. They had character, for the musician had created them with a meaning; but not having been granted as yet a responsive creation in the mind of some other, their life was but a germ. The musically creating and the musically receiving mind must be, as it were, married, else the germs are never recognized, they never come into the children's place. Therefore, the student, looking from his perch, could see these crowding upon the keys of the piano, and hovering about the strings of the violins and violoncello. Here was their orphaned home, and if they wandered it was to return again. Yet they were ever wandering, although they knew that there was no hope, until, indeed, new birth should be granted them, and thus a new chance of life. The air of the room, to one whose ear, like the student's now, could perceive it, was resonant with the murmur of these sounds, longing for life. They had such fine affinities that no discords possibly could occur, for only when they made harmony would they touch each other, otherwise they were repelled and nothing could bring them into contact. Let it not be supposed that they were all pitched in one melancholy key. They moved about in their various characters, yet whether subdued or gay, all alike expressed the one thing lacking to them. They moved, some executing little pirouettes; some in a tender fashion weeping as only little sounds can weep, and glancing across their track came joyous, light-hearted ones. A deep-mouthed one would start from the rendezvous on the violoncello and go rumbling through the air, meeting some fellow from the lower keys of the piano, and they would move in company; on their way they would fall in with a delicate, gossamer-clad sound from the violin, journeying with one like a silver bell in note from the upper keys of the piano. They went mostly in pairs, but many a solitary one kept his own counsel and wandered about whither he would.

The demi-sounds, or those that sought, through human relationship, to ensconce themselves in some palpable form, could see all this, but they could render no help, nor indeed would they leave their tenements, knowing the greater discomforts awaiting them outside. To them the unfortunate ones, shut out from even their imperfect life, were like the spirits who circled about Dante and Virgil in their gloomy visit. It ought before to have been said that in the number of the demi-sounds were found those that had been sent into life through the mimic instruments that made up the orchestra of the Children Symphony which had been performed in the evening. Their abode was humble indeed, but well chosen, for most of them had sought faces of children in simple oil-prints; the Zouave, to be sure, held the one whom the trumpet had sent out, while one awaked by a violin in the same piece, had entered a cabinet picture by Lambdin of a little girl sewing. All of these more perfect sounds possessed so much of the human soul that they could speak indifferently, making use of the mouths they had at command. Such talking was necessarily very imperfect, and to such refined perceptions as sounds have would not have been altogether agreeable; but their aspirations after humanity overbore all objections, and thus quite a conversation was carried on. A neighbor of the student's first addressed him: —

"Meseems, that I have met you before. I am from a sonata of Beethoven myself."

"I recollect you," said the student, "though my ears are rather imperfect. Ah! if I but had the ears which I once possessed I should know you better. For myself I am from the Septuor of Beethoven;" he said this with difficulty, for though his sound-nature held sway, his soul-nature made feeble protest, thinking to itself: "I am denying myself!"

"Then we are connections," said the other, "on the father's side. And yet it seems as if I had other and better knowledge of you. I feel irresistibly drawn toward you."

"It is possible that we have met," replied the student, and now his soul-nature was at least passive. "Your voice has something in it familiar to me." Here spoke the sound that inhabited the portrait in oil of the Professor's grandfather: —

"I am here," said he, "and here I mean to stay. I am from the pitch note of the piano. I was received this evening just long enough to say I was born and then I was dismissed. So I have come here where I can see everything that goes on in the room."

"Hurrah! hurrah! on! charge!"

"What's that? what's that?" asked the student. "I know that voice."

"It's only the Zouave," said the sound that inhabited the portrait of Mozart. "He is near me. I can see him with the great feather behind him. He has broken out before in that fashion. Such a sound has taken possession of him. I am from the tuning of the violin, nor can I expect ever again to find the home that I have been driven from. I have a plan. This has been an unusual evening, and, for a wonder, we are all together still; I propose that we now celebrate our good fortune."

"That pleases me," said the sound that inhabited the portrait of the Professor's grandfather, "and I suggest that each in turn tell his story or sing his song."

"Hurrah! hurrah! on! charge!"

"Do you choose to be quiet!" said the student's neighbor. "Have you no manners? That was a good suggestion. Let us take turns and let the sound that proposed it, being no doubt the oldest, preside and call on each in his place." This was agreed upon, and the sound that inhabited the portrait of the Professor's grandfather, commenced by saying that he had no story to tell. He would have no objections to giving his autobiography but his life had been very uneventful. He could only say that he had tried to live at peace with all; his lot was humble though he came of good family.

When the student heard this he knew not what to think. His soul-nature, feebly as it asserted itself, yet bore witness to a recollection of this same story which it had some time framed. If it could it would have laughed at the coincidence. The sound that dwelt in the portrait of Mozart was now called upon and thus spoke: —

"There was a child that was a dwarf. His father had cast him aside but his mother loved him still. He was the first-born and had his father's face, but most his mother's. Then followed brothers and sisters. He never grew, but they became beautiful youths and maidens, and he was their servant. No one noticed him except for his oddness of appearance, but all praised his brothers and sisters, and rightly, for they were indeed beautiful; and the little dwarf was as pleased as if he himself had been praised. He was a good servant, but no one loved him or cared for him except his mother. His brothers and sisters would never call him brother, yet he was happy."

If the student before was astonished at the coincidence between the words spoken and some past thought or experience of his own, now he was doubly amazed and his soul-nature, rendered curious, was excited so far as its narrow limits allowed, for still his sound-nature prevailed. He said nothing, however, and in its turn spoke a sound that occupied a copy of Palmer's marble Spring. It announced itself as from one of Mendelssohn's songs without words and it did nothing but breathe, yet so sweet was the breath of this sound that each heard for itself a separate song perfectly distinct, and so all were satisfied. The student also heard one, and this also was to him as an old melody.

This is what the sound that dwelt in the image of the Zouave said, even before it was called upon : —

" Hurrah ! the bar of steel is dull in the sun, but the armorer pounds it and shapes it, sharpens it, makes it to shine. Now 'tis a sword ! how it gleams in the sun with its edge so keen ! what shall it cut ?

" The youth and the maiden part at the garden-gate ; she with tears but he with joy ; the sword is his. O brave sword ! has it cut these two ? wait and see.

" Then comes the battle. How the sword fares ! how the enemy fall ! O dashing youth with the brave, bright sword ! all the day long he fights and the good sword glistens.

" Then comes sunset on the battle-field and at the garden-gate. Hurrah ! hurrah ! on ! charge ! "

" That is not well," said the presiding sound. " I thought we should have heard the rest, but you began all over again."

" Is not our turn come ? " asked the children-sounds, and then they told amusing stories: one of how he was overturned in a sleigh; another of going bird's nesting; another of evening sports, and so on. There was great glee over this part, but when they were through, the presiding sound called upon the student's neighbor that had first accosted him, and he spoke in this wise: —

"The snow is on the ground. The sky above is of burnished steel, set with golden stars. My breath stands stiff in the mid air. There is no voice, for the earth is dead and the shroud is on it. The snow is so deep that the grave-stones cannot be seen in the city of the dead. What way of escape is there? The sky is shut tight round the earth. If we dig through the snow the ground is like stone. Shall we climb the steel firmament? Let us try; perchance we may gain the stars. But there is nothing there. Everything is in us. The earth is stone dead and the sky is metal. Let it be so. Is there nothing but winter?"

"That is no story at all," said the presiding sound, "and it is no song, and not at all appropriate. Now let us hear what you have to say, and you shall be the last." And he turned and nodded to the sound that dwelt in the picture of the little girl sewing. "You are to be the last that we will hear, for we cannot be telling stories to each other and singing songs all night. We must stop somewhere, else we may get out of tune, and that is the worst thing that could happen to any sound."

This is what the last and least sound sang: —

The gaunt trees stand
Throughout the land,
And the leaves lie dead at their feet:
The violets' eyes
Are closed likewise,
And the buttercups' lips so sweet.

'Tis early spring;
The woodlands ring
With the shouts of children at play;
They hunt the flowers,
And scatter showers
Of forest leaves by the way.

But death-like sleep
The violets keep,
'Neath the forest leaves stiff and dry;
Yet still the trees,
The sport of the breeze,
Look patiently up to the sky.

Then Heaven descends,
And new life lends
To the gaunt and lonely trees;
And at their feet
Are the violets sweet, —
Their blue eyes — our hearts'-ease.

The student, astonished at the coincidence of the other stories with fancies which he himself had at some time possessed, was more amazed, even to agitation, upon hearing this little song. His memory, which had been excited almost to a human state, assured him that the very words had been composed by him that evening, during the performance of one of the pieces. His mind, affected by all these thoughts, was no longer passive; it struggled with his sound-nature, and a sad and perplexing contest arose. His agitation must have been apparent, for his neighbor, who had frequently addressed him, now spoke: —

"One has been omitted, and one, too, I am convinced, of no ordinary nature. This sound has been housed near me; he is a distant connection, I find, and there is something peculiar about his nature which makes me desire to know more." At this the student-sound could no longer restrain himself, and more to himself than to the rest, gave expression to his disturbed consciousness: —

"I am," he said, "from the Septuor of Beethoven, and if I would, could put my music into words; but I am sadly perplexed since I feel that my life is somewhat more varied and completer than I could thus sing. Whatever I have heard to-night in this little gathering has been old and well known to me. It is as if I had been in turn each who has spoken or sung. I know not why, I am not happy. I feel orphaned; something is lacking." Thus musing, alternately his sound-nature and soul-nature was uppermost. He thought to himself, "If I might but touch the strings of the violin from which I came, I think I should be satisfied." So he slipped out of the figure in the Death-bed of Calvin which he had occupied — the syndic with the handsome leg — and essayed to reach the violin. But there was movement elsewhere also. The various sounds that had contributed to the evening's merry-making, upon hearing the student's voice, recognized, as his neighbor from the first had done, a presence toward which they were drawn. His words had excited in each the same longing, for all felt, even though faintly, that the humanity which it was their highest aspiration again to enter, was present with them, although in a less positive and attractive form than usual. It was in the student's brain, in fact, that each had received that perfection of life which only thus is granted to sounds; the words which they uttered were the product of that union between the music giver's and the music receiver's mind; and it was the dim recollection of having given birth to these fancies that now so perplexed the hapless student-sound. He, once deprived of even the limited corporeity afforded by the figure in the picture, was reduced to a pitiable state; as a sound, he was in part drawn toward the violin, in part, if one might so say, drawn into the soul with which it formed a union; as a soul, craving a union with its body, he was attracted not only to the habitation he had just left, but also — as if it were a great way off — to the more perfect one which preceded. Now, moreover, was he aware of the congregation of sounds vainly seeking him. The rest were indeed moving hither and thither, all in search of the human presence, faintly shadowed to them, assuredly recognized as the complement of their life, but inexplicably vagrant and unattainable. His sound-nature was too controlling to admit of his being revealed to them, and was itself filled with a longing to enter into its own *alter ego*, the soul-nature: *that* was degraded and almost powerless, because it had disengaged itself from its natural tenement. But struggling is so much opposed to the nature of sound, which is passive, that his soul grew more and more conscious of its powers; the memory grew stronger, and he thought: —

"How insufficient my abode in the figure of the picture was. I was indeed a sound as I now am, but I could see little and hear little. I had fine affinities, it is true, with other sounds, yet they lacked much that I have possessed. It was like a dream and seemed unreal. But I can remember how once — it was long ago — I had larger life. I lived in a student. I was not thus beaten about, homeless and unsatisfied. I was housed in a noble body that had sensibility and fineness of vision, and hearing and scent. O, that I might once more be in my old home!"

This wish also was energetic; the sound shrank to its proportional measure while the soul became enlarged and was borne by its fervent wish toward its old seat. As it passed out, it was aware, by its still musical affinity, of the aspiration ever growing fainter to it, though in reality more earnest, of the congregation of sounds within praying to be allowed to accompany it. Fragments of melodies entered for a moment the soul, but were not retained. Doubtless these followed still, long after it was conscious of their presence. Itself, as before, found its way through the key-hole, and entered as mysteriously as it had left the body of the student, which was standing upright on the door-step, the right hand buttoning the upper button of the great-coat, while the head was turned upward toward the moon.

Immediately upon the entry of the soul, the hand finished its task, and the head was bent down. The student walked cautiously down the steps. "That air runs in my head still," said he, and he whistled it. "That is better," thought the sound, as well as it could think: "it is like a new creation."

## WOLFGANG AMADEUS MOZART.

It has often been observed that a child of great parts proves in the end to be a man of only ordinary capacity, and it has become common to look with distrust upon precocious children, as likely to disappoint their guardians and friends, either by not growing up at all, or by leaving behind with their youth all that made them remarkable. But Mozart the musician was plainly an exception to these examples ; for he not only had a wonderful genius in music when a mere child, so that he bore comparison with masters in the art, but his genius never forsook him, expanding with his years, until he stood the most eminent of musical artists of his time, and only to be mentioned now in company with the truly great men whose works give us the law in musical matters.

His father, Leopold Mozart, was a musician who stood high in the employ of the Archbishop of Salzburg, a town lying between Munich and Vienna. He was an educated

man, but being forced to gain a livelihood through the practice of music, he became, like most of that profession in those days, dependent upon the favor of some person of distinction, either in church or state. Accordingly, he was in the service of the Archbishop, and occupied the position of Hof-Kapellmeister, conductor of the court music. He had two children, Wolfgang, and Maria Anna, or Nannerl, as she was called, who was four or five years older. When Nannerl was seven years old her father began to teach her music upon the clavier, an instrument of which the piano-forte of the present day is an improved form. She learned very rapidly, and showed a remarkable genius for reading and executing music. But while she was taking her lessons, there appeared a greater, in her little brother Wolfgang, then not more than three years old, who stood by her, and would himself strike the keys, but never, like most children, in sport, striking at hap-hazard, and only pounding to bring some sound out; for he was pained by discords, and would only strike harmoniously. Indeed, scarcely had he begun to express himself like other intelligent children, by words and meaning actions, before he showed that he had much music in him that would come out. He would catch quickly what was played to him, and play it correctly himself; he would even invent little pieces, which he played; and his very sports were set to music, for when he was playing with his favorite, a trumpeter in his father's band, he would insist that the playthings should be carried from one room to another to the sound of music. He was an affectionate little fellow, full of tenderness, and eager to be loved; so that he would jump up from his sports and run to those about him, asking if they really loved him; if they laughed and teased him by saying No, his eyes would fill with tears.

There was one other study besides music which took hold of him, and that was arithmetic. The floors, and walls, and chairs, and tables were covered with figures which the impulsive little scholar was using; and this is not to be wondered at, for though music seems to us often such a matter of feeling, yet we know that the science of music is very exact, and has much to do with numbers, as any one may see who notices such expressions as thirds, consecutive fifths, and the like.

As little Wolfgang grew, his father and all looked on in wonder. It seemed as if they could teach him nothing, for whatever they told him of music, that he seemed to know already. Nevertheless the boy studied hard, practicing and composing, and led a happy life between his clavier, his figures, and his childish plays; they all seemed to be the same thing. When he was seated at the instrument he was like one in sport, and when he was busy with his games he was like one in earnest, so natural and fresh was his life. At length, when he was six years old and Nannerl eleven, his father, who had for many months given up teaching music to others that he might educate his children, determined to take a journey with them, and show the world how wonderful they were, especially his little Wolfgang. At that time a musician, if he would prosper, must attach himself to some prince, or other person of distinction; and if he was dissatisfied with his place, he must travel and seek some other patron. Mozart, the father, was not contented at Salzburg, and he wished to try his fortunes elsewhere; he wished also by travel to teach the children many things, and to bring them to the knowledge of such persons as would be likely to notice and help them. They took short journeys first, to Munich and Vienna, and encouraged by the great attention which they received, they set out on a tour which occupied them three years, during which they visited Paris and London, and travelled through Germany, Holland, France, and Switzerland, the father all the while carefully educating his children. On this tour the children performed wherever there was a court, — Wolfgang playing the clavier, the organ, and the violin; singing, playing, and composing extempore; and indeed, doing at eight or nine years, all the various things which are done by educated musicians.

Everybody was astonished at the child, and every one loved him; for little Wolfgang, while playing the most difficult music, was only doing what it was easy and natural for him to do, and he would go right from his music to his sports as if they were both alike to him. When he was in England, he was playing before a gentleman who tells how "While playing to me, a favorite cat came in, on which he left his harpsichord, nor could we bring him back for a considerable time. He would also run about the room with a stick between his legs by way of horse." Wherever they went they were treated with attention, and presents were given them, after the fashion of the day, not only in money, but in the shape of snuff-boxes, watches, and elegant clothes.

When they were once more in Salzburg, the troubles which always gather about reputation, began to arise. The Archbishop, who was wont to think of the musicians as his servants, was annoyed that they should be receiving honor and renown of which he had small share, and resolved that they should be still more dependent upon him; and the other musicians began to be filled with a mean jealousy of this wonderful boy, and they did all they could to make him seem less remarkable. They kept out of his way and refused to hear him play, in order that, when they were asked about him, they might say, "O, we have never heard him; we do not wish to encourage a mountebank," knowing very well that they could not thus speak of him after hearing him; but the father laid a trap for one of them.

"I had persuaded some one, quietly," he says, "to give us intelligence when he would be present, and our friend was to bring this person an extraordinary difficult concerto, which could be placed before little Wolfgang. We came together, and he had the opportunity of hearing his concerto played by Wolfgang, as if he knew it by heart. The astonishment of this composer and clavier-player, and the expressions of admiration he used, confirmed all that I have stated above. He ended by saying, 'I can say no less, as an honest man, than that this boy is the greatest man in the world; it could not have been believed.'"

Still Mozart kept on studying and composing, growing more admirable as a musician every day, and keeping, too, just as boyish and full of life and merriment. He did not mind these things as his father did, who now began to lay plans for Wolfgang, that he might be freed from the necessity of living always at Salzburg. The two took a journey to Italy, and Wolfgang, who was now nearly fifteen years old, gave himself up to the life about him; he wrote music, he heard music, he visited friends who covered him with favors, and in the midst of all he was constantly writing letters home, full of fun and merry wisdom. At Milan his first opera, "Mithridates," was performed, and brought the most triumphant applause. It was church music, however, which at that time he wrote best and most freely.

For ten years now, Mozart continued to live in Salzburg, and to make journeys thence, with shifting fortune, but always pouring out his wonderful music, and suffering no trials or vexations to drive him from freely using the gift which God had bestowed upon him. But at twenty-five he was called to Munich to compose an opera, and to this he gave himself heart and soul. It was "Idomeneus, King of Crete," and Mozart, in the strength of his young manhood, produced in this opera something new; for though other operas had been written before it, this, written in a few weeks, is the "basis of all the music of our day." It brought him friends, and filled the young composer with high hope of a future career, unchecked by the petty tyranny of the Archbishop of Salzburg. "I should rejoice," he writes to his father at this time, "were I to be told that my services were no longer required; for with the great patronage that I have here, both my present and future circumstances would be secure, death excepted, which no one can guard against, though no great misfortune to a single man. But anything in the world to please you. It would be less trying to me if I could only occasionally escape from time to time, just to draw my breath. You know how difficult it was to get away on this occasion; and without some very urgent cause, there would not be the faintest hope of such a thing. It is enough to make one weep to think of it, so I say no more."

His father and Nannerl visited Munich to hear the opera. In the midst of festivities came a command from the Archbishop for Mozart to accompany his household to Vienna, for the prelate wished to appear in great pomp in the Imperial city. Mozart obeyed the summons, and thenceforth his life was led there, for he never returned to Salzburg to live. It gives an idea of the dependent life which a musician led, though he were a man of divine genius, when we read in one of Mozart's letters, written just after reaching Vienna: "Our party consists of the two valets, the comptroller, Herr Zetti, the confectioner, the two cooks, Cecarelli, Brunetti, and my insignificant self. N. B. — The two valets sit at the head of the table. I have, at all events, the honor to be placed above the cooks; I almost believe I am back in Salzburg! At table all kinds of coarse, silly joking go on; but no one jokes with me, for I never say a word, or, if I am obliged to speak, I do so with the utmost gravity, and when I have dined I go away." To be reckoned by the Archbishop as a fit companion for his valets and cooks! But Mozart shows in his words that though he sat at table with them he would not make himself their comrade. It was evident that the Archbishop consulted only his own vanity, and Mozart very shortly determined to cut loose from the service. To do this was hard, for it was also to disobey his father, who trembled before the Archbishop's power. Mozart had ever been a boy in his filial obedience, and now when he took this step contrary to his father's wishes, but impelled by the keenest sense of honor and self-respect, he grew, as we think, suddenly a man. He seemed to his friends to be plunging into ruin, but in reality he was now just entering upon his great career. He married shortly after, and threw himself for support on teaching and composition.

Now succeeded ten years of busy life. All varieties of musical compositions came thick and fast from his pen. The most dramatic of musical romances, — "Don Giovanni," that fanciful and sweet play, "The Magic Flute," and his symphonies that flow like changing streams through woods and sunlit fields, — were products of this period. His life was brimming with music and social pleasure. Care and anxiety indeed came upon him; with manhood he left off some of his youthful exuberance of spirit, and until the end he seemed always at odds with riches, never free from petty embarrassment, but more than once there is an April scene of sun and rain chasing one another in his familiar letters. Listen to him as he adds a postscript to a letter to his absent wife: "While writing the last page, many a tear has fallen on it. But now let us be merry. Look! Swarms of kisses are flying about — quick! catch some! I have caught three, and delicious they are. . . . . Adieu, my dearest, sweetest wife! Be careful of your health, and do not go into the town on foot. Write to me how you like your new quarters. Adieu! I send you a million kisses!" And again in another postscript, "Kiss Sophie for me. To Silsmag (his little boy) I send two good fillips on the nose, and a hearty pull at his hair. A thousand compliments to Stoll. Adieu! 'The hour strikes! Farewell! We shall meet again!'"

These words were the last written by him; they are quoted from the "Magic Flute," on which he was then engaged. They intimate what was passing in his mind, for the shadow of death was creeping over him. Some time before, a tall man, clad in sombre gray, had called upon him to inquire whether he would undertake to write a Requiem, but did not name the person who ordered it. Mozart accepted the order, and set about it eagerly; but before finishing it, was forced to visit Prague. Just as he was setting out, the mysterious man in gray appeared suddenly by the carriage to demand the "Requiem." There was something singular about his manner, and that, taken with the subject — a funeral piece — took strong hold of Mozart, and he gave himself up to the task. We know now that all the mystery was due to the wish of a certain count to get possession of this "Requiem," and to pass himself off as the composer. But Mozart was conscious of an ebb in his life. Long before others would believe it, and before any visible sign was seen beyond a weariness under the cares and labors imposed upon him, he saw the approaching end, and declared that he was writing this "Requiem" for his own funeral. Gradually his strength failed, as he worked upon it, and he could not leave the house. Then he could not leave his bed; but still he labored, hoping to complete it as a final account of his life; and so he did in every material point. "In it," says his biographer, "he expressed, in never-dying powerful tones, his consciousness of guilt, and of reconciliation with Heaven. In the innermost depths of his heart he was conscious of his human frailty, and expressed the deep penitence of his heart in chords such as no mortal ear had ever yet heard. It was also a great consolation to him to remember that the Lord, to whom he had drawn near in humble and child-like faith, had suffered and died for him, and would look on him in love and compassion. The day before his death, he desired the score to be brought to him in bed (it was two o'clock in the afternoon), and sang his part; others took the soprano, tenor, and bass. They had got through the various parts, to the first bars of the *Lacrimosa,* when Mozart suddenly burst into tears, and laid aside the score. The delicate organs of his bodily frame were already fast decaying, so that even his cherished canary was obliged to be taken out of the room, because the invalid could no longer bear its singing."

His wife's sister has written of his dying days: "The last movement of his life was an endeavor to indicate where the kettle-drums should be used in his 'Requiem.' I think I still hear the sound." Another messenger than the tall man in gray had come, even Death, and so Mozart was borne away in his thirty-fifth year. But his life on earth was finished. There remain many letters by himself and others, from which we know something of his daily life; above all, we still hear his music sounding forth. It can never die. He moved through the mean things of life like a divine being. He obeyed the voice from on high which perpetually bade him sing! He was music itself, ever youthful, — full of heavenly harmony.

## THE RETURN OF ORPHEUS.

When the world was young Orpheus sang to it, and when the world grew old, Orpheus came again and sang a second time. At the first visit all were so enchanted that the rocks and trees could not sit still, but jumped up and danced about to the sound of the music. That was when the world was young and foolish; no one was looking on and all did as they pleased. When the world grew old, it was wiser and did nothing without thinking about it, and asking what its ancestors would have thought, what its posterity was going to think.

Now it was whispered about that Orpheus was to revisit the world. The world had not forgotten his first coming; the Evergreens took care of that. They stood sprinkled in the forest and though the rest slept, they kept awake, — they never forgot. All that had happened was intrusted to them to remember. Each year in the spring, they told of Orpheus' visit, and at last, one spring, they added: "He is now to come again, for when he left us he promised to return when the blood of heroes should make the cold world warm enough for his footsteps."

The rocks, the trees, the bushes, all heard this and expected Orpheus, but they were not quite certain how they ought to behave. "When the world was young," they said, "our ancestors danced, very likely, but the question is — are *we* to dance? A great deal has happened since those days; all sorts of fiddlers have been fiddling, singers have been singing, there has been no general dance, one or two may have skipped a little, but they make no rule; if reports are correct, they were not always very reputable." This was the common talk, but the matter was so interesting that there were many separate opinions.

"What think you, neighbor?" asked the Elm of the Oak. "Shall we dance?"

"Shall we stand on our heads?" growled the Oak; "I have a better opinion of myself than to think I shall engage in such foolery," and he thrust his knobby arms out and dug himself deeper into the earth, for he meant to get such a hold and make such a solid stand that he never should be shaken.

"I see nothing to dance for," said the Willow; "I can't dry my tears so suddenly for every strolling player that chooses to pipe for me."

"It is undignified to dance," said the Poplar. "How I should look!"

"Well, I should like to dance pretty well," said the Elm; "it is graceful exercise, but then I don't care about it if the rest do not dance. I should not wish to be conspicuous."

The Rocks said they would dance; they only asked that Orpheus should play loud enough to move them, and that he should play exactly as he did when he came before. They were perfectly willing to dance, but they must insist on knowing the tune. The Evergreens said they should dance, as a matter of course; it would be ridiculous not to; they were ready, only let him come and strike up — they would lead off.

Orpheus came with his lyre and sang. The Evergreens immediately began to dance, but they were out of time from beginning to end. It was not the music that made them dance; in fact, they led off before Orpheus had uttered a note. When the Elm saw them she also began to dance quite gracefully, though she did not listen much to the music. But she saw the Oak clinching his knobby fists at Orpheus, and she stopped, pretending that she had only been practicing some steps by herself, which was true. The Willow had her griefs, and she said, "'Tis better to sigh than be dancing." The Poplar cried, "Hem!" and looked serious; he was not quite sure about this dancing. The Rocks were covered with lichens hundreds of years old, and they said, —

"This is very different music from what moved our ancestors. We know about that music; we have reduced it to perfect rules. Keep to the rules and we will dance; not otherwise," and they sat stiff.

Orpheus wept. "Will no one listen?" he cried. "The ground is wet with the blood of heroes, and I sing their souls into life." Once more he touched his lyre and sang with sweeter power. There was a stir in the forest. The shoots that had lately sprung from the earth, miniature trees, having the perfect structure folded in their tiny forms, whirled in the joyous dance. The rocks that peeped from the soil joined carefully in the movement. The earth trembled with excitement. Above all sounded the clear voice of Orpheus singing to his lyre. He turned away from the old and sang to the new. He sang and the world grew young again; the young shoots sprang up and waved their branches; the flowers opened their cups, and the sun filled them with golden light; the air was fragrant with music.

A new song had been sung, a new dance had been led, and when all was at the height Orpheus fled; but the world was young again. Will it ever be different?

# BEFORE THE FIRE.

## "AS GOOD AS A PLAY."

THERE was quite a row of them on the mantel-piece. They were all facing front, and it looked as if they had come out of the wall behind, and were on their little stage facing the audience. There was the bronze monk reading a book by the light of a candle, who had a private opening under his girdle, so that sometimes his head was thrown violently back, and one looked down into him and found him full of brimstone matches. Then the little boy leaning against a greyhound; he was made of Parian, very fine Parian too, so that one would expect to find a glass cover over him: but no; the glass cover stood over a cat, and a cat made of worsted too: still it was a very old cat, fifty years old in fact. There was another young person there, young like the boy leaning on a greyhound, and she too was of Parian: she was very fair in front, but behind, — ah, that is a secret which it is not quite time yet to tell. One other stood there, at least she seemed to stand, but nobody could see her feet, for her dress was so very wide and so finely flounced. She was the china girl that rose out of a pen-wiper.

The fire in the grate below was of soft coal, and flashed up and down, throwing little jets of flame up that made very pretty foot-lights. So here was a stage, and here were the actors, but where was the audience? O, the Audience was in the arm-chair in front. He had a special seat; he was a critic, and could get up when he wanted to, when the play became tiresome, and go out.

"It is painful to say such things out loud," said the Boy-leaning-against-a-greyhound, with a trembling voice, "but we have been together so long, and these people round us never will go away. Dear girl, will you? — you know." It was the Parian girl that he spoke to, but he did not look at her; he could not, he was leaning against the greyhound; he only looked at the Audience.

"I am not quite sure," she coughed. "If now you were under a glass-case."

"I am under a glass-case," spoke up the Cat-made-of-worsted. "Marry me. I am fifty years old. Marry me, and live under a glass-case."

"Shocking!" said she. "How can you? Fifty years old, too! That would indeed be a match!"

"Marry!" muttered the bronze Monk-reading-a-book. "A match! I am full of matches, but I don't marry. Folly!"

"You stand up very straight, neighbor," said the Cat-made-of-worsted.

"I never bend," said the bronze Monk-reading-a-book. "Life is earnest. I read a book by a candle. I am never idle."

The Cat-made-of-worsted grinned to himself.

"You've got a hinge in your back," said he. "They open you in the middle; your head flies back. How the blood must run down. And then you're full of brimstone matches. He! he!" and the Cat-made-of-worsted grinned out loud. The Boy-leaning-against-a-greyhound spoke again, and sighed, —

"I am of Parian, you know, and there is no one else here of Parian, except yourself."

"And the greyhound," said the Parian girl.

"Yes, and the greyhound," said he, eagerly. "He belongs to me. Come, a glass-case is nothing to it. We could roam; O, we could roam!"

"I don't like roaming."

"Then we could stay at home, and lean against the greyhound."

"No," said the Parian girl, "I don't like that."

"Why?"

"I have private reasons."

"What?"

"No matter."

"I know," said the Cat-made-of-worsted. "I saw her behind. She's hollow. She's stuffed with lamp-lighters. He! he!" and the Cat-made-of-worsted grinned again.

"I love you just as much," said the steadfast Boy-leaning-against-a-greyhound, "and I don't believe the Cat."

"Go away," said the Parian girl, angrily. "You're all hateful. I won't have you."

"Ah!" sighed the Boy-leaning-against-a-greyhound.

"Ah!" came another sigh, — it was from the China-girl-rising-out-of-a-pen-wiper, — "how I pity you."

"Do you?" said he, eagerly. "Do you? Then I love you. Will you marry me?"

"Ah!" said she; "but" —

"She can't!" said the Cat-made-of-worsted. "She can't come to you. She hasn't got any legs. I know it. I'm fifty years old. I never saw them."

"Never mind the Cat," said the Boy-leaning-against-a-greyhound.

"But I do mind the Cat," said she, weeping. "I haven't. It's all pen-wiper."

"Do I care?" said he.

"She has thoughts," said the bronze Monk-reading-a-book. "That lasts longer than beauty. And she is solid behind."

"And she has no hinge in her back," grinned the Cat-made-of-worsted. "Come, neighbors, let us congratulate them. You begin."

"Keep out of disagreeable company," said the bronze Monk-reading-a-book.

"That is not congratulation; that is advice," said the Cat-made-of-worsted. "Never mind, go on, my dear," — to the Parian girl. "What! nothing to say? Then I'll say it for you. 'Friends, may your love last as long as your courtship.' Now I'll congratulate you."

But before he could speak, the Audience got up.

"You shall not say a word. It must end happily."

He went to the mantel-piece and took up the China-girl-rising-out-of-a-pen-wiper.

"Why, she has legs after all," said he.

"They're false," said the Cat-made-of-worsted. "They're false. I know it. I'm fifty years old. I never saw true ones on her."

The Audience paid no attention, but took up the Boy-leaning-against-a-greyhound.

"Ha!" said the Cat-made-of-worsted, "Come. I like this. He's hollow. They're all hollow. He! he! Neighbor Monk, you're hollow. He! he!" and the Cat-made-of-worsted never stopped grinning. The Audience lifted the glass-case from him and set it over the Boy-leaning-against-a-greyhound and the China-girl-rising-out-of-a-pen-wiper.

"Be happy!" said he.

"Happy!" said the Cat-made-of-worsted. "Happy!"

Still they were happy.

## THE ENCHANTMENT OF OLD DANIEL.

In the White Mountain district of New England, high up among the hills, is a little valley, so retired that scarce any but enthusiastic trout-hunters have found it out, and so lonely that one sees here and there deserted farms, whose occupants had not courage to stay in the solitude, but have fled to busier haunts. Mount Osceola looks down upon it, overtopping a company of hills that shoulder each other, and Mad River tumbles headlong out of the valley, rushing into the dark pine woods. Thick forests are all about, and it would seem a gloomy place to enter at nightfall, with only one or two twinkling lights in the one or two houses, and the white road making its way to the little saw-mill, which stands in a niche, carved out of the black woods, at the further end of the valley. Gloomier still would it seem to push by the mill into the silent woods, following a foot-path little used, and feeling the forest close behind one, as if shutting out forever the light of day and the voices of men.

Yet, along this lonely path, leaving the mill behind and going deeper into the forest, walked an old man, with a bag on his back, upon the night of the last day of the year. It was Daniel Desmond, a hoary-headed mariner, who for fifty years had followed the sea, being shifted with his battered chest from one vessel to another, sailing north, south, east, and west, and had at last given up the pursuit, mooring his old hulk at the foot of Mount Osceola, in the loneliest spot of the lonely valley of the Mad. For, back from the valley, was a clearing in the forest which had been made long years before by a man who thought it as good and cheap a place as any in which to work and live. He had built a small house there, had planted a field, and put up a fence to keep out the world and the world's stray cattle; but the place grew to be so utterly desolate that at length he fled from it, leaving the house and ploughed field and fences to be inhabited by the squirrels, or perchance by bears and bob-cats. So it had remained for several years. The forest, seeing no one about, began by degrees to resume its claim to the land which had been forcibly taken from it. First the little trees came timidly across the edge of the clearing, and, finding no one, not even a scarecrow in the corn-field, they made up their minds to stay; then the trees behind pushed them forward, and so the forest again began to take possession of the clearing, while the rain and wind and the hot sun all attacked the helpless house, till it began to crumble.

It was to this forlorn spot that old Daniel was slowly making his way along the wood-path. It was dark above, for heavy clouds were in the sky; it was dark all about, so that he could scarcely make out the path with his eyes; and it was darker than all in poor old Daniel's heart. For that afternoon his shaggy dog, Lion, sole house-companion, had strayed away, whither he knew not. He stopped now and then to whistle for his dog, but whistled and waited in vain. He did not find him at home either when he reached the crumbling house, which he was making shift to live in; and Daniel shook his head miserably all the evening as he crouched over his fire, which warmed his old bones, to be sure, but seemed unable to send a particle of warmth into his shivering soul.

But why was this battered mariner ending his days in such forlorn fashion, and what miserable fortune drove him to this lonely spot? An idle reason indeed: but nothing better could old Daniel answer, than that in this valley he was born and here he spent his childhood; that, when he went away to be beaten about on seas, he carried with him a blessed memory of the spot, and ever his one dream had been — whether frozen in the northern ice, or tossed in torrid zone — to come back to his New England home and end his days in the valley of the Mad. So he had come, and here he was living in the old house which his father had built and fled from, and where his childish memories clustered. It was not so beautiful as he remembered it; but he clung to it like the shipwrecked mariner he was, flung up into these hills from the tossing sea.

As old Daniel sat by the fire, rubbing his hands slowly over his head, he began to think of his voyages, of the strange lands he had seen. Everywhere that he had been, to be sure, he had thought it not half so beautiful as the little home on the mountains; but somehow, now that he was here, the old man was restless to be elsewhere. He went to the window and looked out, shading his face with his hands. Nothing to be seen; it was all black, and there was no sign of faithful Lion.

"Dear, dear," he sighed to himself, "if only I could take one voyage more and sail to some new land, where all this trouble should be gone, and things wouldn't be quite so black and dismal. O, this is a doleful New Year's Eve. It don't look as if the new year were going to be much better than the old ones," and Daniel fumbled about the room with his tallow candle, putting things to rights before he should go to bed. Even when he had gathered himself up for a night's sleep, he continued to shake his head, and mumble over the forlorn world which he had to live in, when he was sure there was one somewhere which was bright and pure.

But where was the bark that would sail to such a world, and take in such a weather-beaten, dreary fellow? If Daniel had been asked, he would have shaken his head more dolefully than before, and yet near it was; and now indeed began a wonder. The mariner had shut his eyes upon the old earth with its leafless trees and dingy ground, its gloomy forests hemming in the open clearing, and the open clearing itself, with its stubble and decayed stumps and rotten fences. All that was out of sight, not to be wished back; something better was to come, and that right soon. For now there came, without sound, but filling the place with light, a ship of silver, crescent-shaped, without mast or sails or rudder, and yet floating on the air, close by the hoary-headed mariner.

"Come! sail with us, Daniel," he heard from a voice, and wondering, but nothing loth, old Daniel stepped aboard and away sailed the silver ship through the air. He was not alone; for as he sat, feeling a gentle warmth steal through him there, he saw bright figures all about, and one, more beautiful than the rest, who had called him to the ship and now stood beside him. It was Neonetta, the fairy of New Year's night; this was her silver ship, and these her attendants. The light grew brighter, and Daniel's eyes got more open, for everything now was distinct. They had left the dingy earth; that and the old year had gone off together; they were sailing over a sea of cloud which lay in billows beneath, while above the bright stars were shining. There was no wind to chill, and yet the ship sped on, cutting her way over the billowy clouds.

But what were all the little attendants doing? Wonderful works they were at, to be sure, for, looking behind, Daniel saw a bright train of them, reaching over the ship's side and receiving from little hands glittering balls of every hue; they tossed them as if in merry sport, and a shower of the balls shot across the silver ship. But beyond in the prow was another train of bright fairies, leaning over the side and flinging down the balls into the deep. Once, looking at the wake, the clouds parted, and Daniel saw that the train reached far down in a brilliant flowing line; he could see them flinging up the little balls, which grew brighter and brighter as they neared the ship; but, strange to say, as they shot along to the fairies at the prow, they clung together, and, from glittering balls of every hue, they became starry forms of pure white. "These are the white star-makers," said Neonetta, smiling, as old Daniel looked wonderingly at her. "They are busy now, for we are sailing to a new land, in which I am to be queen, and the white stars are to decorate the country. Are you not weary of the old earth and the bare trees and ragged ground?" Daniel nodded vehemently. "Yes, yes," he mumbled, but could not hear himself speak. "Well," she continued, "that is gone. I knew you were weary of it, and so I am taking you to my home. O, it will be glorious there, so pure and still!" The little lady waved her hands and faster flew the bright balls, while the white stars danced through the air, as if they, too, were glad.

"What house shall we live in, Daniel?" asked Neonetta, dancing about him. "Shall it be in one with shining spires and glittering domes, with stars for windows and crystals for doors?"

"Let us have a good fire," mumbled Daniel, who at this moment felt the wind from Neonetta's robe.

"No, no," she cried, looking faint; "but we will have a soft white carpet, and, when we walk abroad, soft white mantles over our shoulders. But what shall we have to eat, Daniel? We will pluck the boughs and shake off the sweet fruit that grows on the evergreen. And then the music and the pictures! Music so sweet, that it is like the chiming of distant bells, and such pictures as never were seen on the old, dingy earth." Again the little lady flung up her tiny arms, and danced over the silver ship. Faster flew the white stars, and the long train of fairies ascended and descended in a flowing line of changing light. The silver ship sped on, and now the billowy clouds grew thinner, while above, the stars that had shone, one by one went out before a clearer light which began to spread and spread over the sky.

"The new land!" cried Neonetta, dancing

about old Daniel, who was now peering over the ship's side. "Come with me out of my silver ship," and she reached her hand to him. He looked around: the shining fairies had vanished, but Neonetta was by him. He looked once more. Neonetta was gone, and at the same moment vanished the silver ship. Old Daniel sprang up. It was dark about him, but his old legs bore him, half groping, toward an opening of light. He looked beyond, and there, far away in the distant sky, was sailing the silver ship, now turned to gold. In crescent form, it was floating in the air and sailing away, away, growing fainter and fainter. He looked about him, and found himself in the new land, for instead of the old, dingy earth, there was a pure, white soil, stretching away in gentle ridges. Instead of the naked trees, which he had left in all their dismal barrenness, here were fair trees, laden with white foliage, their boughs weighed down with the heavy white fruit. He turned and looked behind him. There stood a little house, all dressed in white, with a white robe flung over it, that hung down from the roof and over the window top. He looked above and beyond. A mountain raised itself, like a good old man, with splendid brow; while a forest spread around, like a great company of beautiful maidens clad in snowy white.

The air was still, when a chickadee set up its little note of cheer and welcome. Far off he heard a wagon, with its load of wood. As it moved over the new soil, a blissful sound rose in the air, as if in this new land all toil was sweet with music. Then, better still, he heard a distant baying. Ho, ho! it cried, like a clear bell; ho, ho! nearer still, coming through the forest. Old Daniel looked again for the silver ship turned golden, but it had gone, and in its place bright colors of rose and violet filled the sky, as if no clouds were to hang over this beautiful earth, but glad hues of every kind. He listened still, and heard now the voice of Neonetta calling to him in the distance. "Come!" she cried, "ere it is too late;" and the voice, even while she spake, grew fainter. "Ho, ho!" sounded the baying, nearer now and nearer. "Come!" cried Neonetta, in faint tones. "Ho, ho! — ho, ho!"

Only a moment more, Queen Neonetta! for thy enchantment over Daniel. The sun will rise, the cock will crow, good Lion will bound across the snow-covered clearing. But, we will not stay. Hark! there is Lion again. Ho, ho!

## THE NEIGHBORS.

When Christmas comes in the winter-time, as it has come ever since I can remember, the earth is very apt to get a Christmas present of a fall of snow; and if one were an old fence, or a house-roof, or a patch of brown dry grass that had once been green, one would wish every Christmas to have the same present of a great snow fall that should cover one up, so that people would say, — "Really, how charmingly that old fence looks;" or "How the snow takes off the sharpness of that roof;" or, if they were trying to be poetical, "See what a soft ermine mantle hangs over the shoulder of that hill!" And yet, if the snow lay heavily upon the house-roof very long, one would think that there could be little heat for the dwellers inside, else it would be melted off.

Everybody, however, does not keep a fire burning all night in the house, and perhaps that was the reason why two houses which stood almost touching each other had heavy capes of snow on, the night before Christmas. It was easily to be seen, for the moon was shining brightly after the day's snow-storm, and the house-tops looked wonderfully white and cold. These two houses, though the snow fell on both alike, were as different as two men. One, with its pointed roof, was like a tall man with an old-fashioned hat on. It stood in a dignified sort of way, as if it respected itself, looking out in every direction with windows set firmly in their places, or perched, leaning upon their elbows, on the roof. Each of the windows had its own private cap, which it kept on all the while of course, for its head was out-of-doors in all kinds of weather; and the front door had, besides, two pillars on which to lean. A flight of steps led up to it, so that people who wished to enter must climb up to it, and ring a brass bell-handle, and read FROME on a great door-plate. There was a chimney, with a row of little chimney-pots on top — a separate little hole for each fire-place in the house: the range in the kitchen sent up its smoke by a sort of private back-stairs, so as not to interfere with the smoke from the parlor and the dining-room. And the fence in front of the house had a brass head on each iron spike, and they stood in a row, glaring at one like a squad of policemen, saying, "Keep your hands off the house, if they're not clean!"

It seems very strange, then, that upon one side of this house the windows should all look at the wall of the other house, which stood separated from it by not more than ten feet. They did not indeed look into it, for their blinds were all shut tight, but it was for no lack of openness in the other house. This had no blinds at all, and it had windows directly opposite the blinds, at which they stared all day long, like eyes without winkers. The house was not so high, however, as Mr. Frome's, and had a flat roof, over which the upper windows in the roof of Mr. Frome's house could see very well if there was anything worth looking at. It was a squarish, short-necked house, sitting on the ground, and one could walk straight in by a door so flat that when it was shut one could hardly tell it from the rest of the house-front. Regular rows of windows occupied the front and side, looking as if they had all been sawed out after the house was made. There was no fence in front; but the fence that separated it from the neighbor house was right against this house, or rather the house looked as if it had been set against the fence, for the fence was older. There was a name upon the door, spelled in china letters — GRASH. So Mr. Grash lived here.

At the time when our story begins there was no light in Mr. Frome's house, but in a window of the second story of Mr. Grash's there was a twinkling light, and shadows of persons could be seen moving back and forth. There was a light in the neighboring room also. It was nearly midnight; the snow-storm which had fallen all day had given place to bright moonlight, but clouds had gathered, and there was promise of a new snow-storm. Nevertheless, two humble neighbors that had come out to see each other in the moonlight, remained out-of-doors. They were two cats, upon the roofs of these two houses. One was sitting on the sill of a roof-window of Mr. Frome's house — that was Mr. Frome's Cat; the other was upon the roof of Mr. Grash's house — that was Mr. Grash's Cat. They could talk very easily across the narrow space that separated the two houses.

"A still night, neighbor," said Mr. Frome's Cat.

"Aye, you may well say that," rejoined Mr. Grash's Cat. "This snow does make soft travelling. It's the only time when I wish I were white, — snow-white I mean, for I have some white," and he looked proudly on his fur. "One makes dreadful shadows on the snow. I say, do you think we should make less if we were wholly white?"

"Well, I am not sure," said the other, reflecting. "But it's the moon you know that makes us make shadows, and this is what puzzles me. Why does not the moon make a shadow too? That great round thing goes across the sky as fast as a rat sometimes, but we don't see any round shadow going down the street. I've often watched for it," and he looked puzzled. They both sat some time in silence, but neither could answer the question. Mr. Frome's Cat was still thinking about it, but Mr. Grash's Cat had other thoughts. He spoke again, —

"I say, does she ever leave the cover off?"

"The cover?"

"Yes, the cover; you know, the cook, in the back-yard," said Mr. Grash's Cat, licking his chops, and looking rather hungry.

"I am fed in the house," said Mr. Frome's Cat with dignity.

"As if you did not go out and help yourself," said the other scornfully.

"I have no need to," said Mr. Frome's Cat coldly, "and we don't keep it in the yard."

"Don't tell me! precious fine you are with your wall behind, so high I can't climb over. How some people think they're too good for their neighbors!" and Mr. Grash's Cat looked spitefully across.

"Our neighbors were not of our choosing," said Mr. Frome's Cat. "We hardly should select such ungenerous — but, O dear! I knew we should quarrel if we got on to this subject again. Come, it has begun to snow again, let us part."

"Ungenerous!" exclaimed Mr. Grash's Cat, — "ungenerous! is not this our land, and did we not have the right to build just where we pleased on our own land? and if your house happened to stand so near, say, was that our fault? and if your windows looked into ours on one side, say, did we make your windows? Ungenerous!"

"But, Mr. Grash," said Mr. Frome's Cat, — they always called each other Mr. Frome and Mr. Grash when they got excited talking about the houses, — "but, Mr. Grash, our house was built first" —

"And could no one else build a house after you, good Mr. Frome?"

"Nay, hear me, friend Grash. We built our house first when there was no other house near, and put windows upon this side purposely to see the fine view beyond. We tried to buy your land, but you would not sell, and said you had no thought of building; and then because you claimed that our fence was set a half foot on your ground, though the law showed it was not, what should you do but out of spite build a house on the very edge of your land, shutting out our view on that side and obliging us to close all the windows. I must say it was ungenerous; it was more, it was wicked!" and Mr. Frome's Cat held up his paw and looked the other way.

"O, O!" snarled Mr. Grash's Cat, "and you are the upright, honest neighbor that went to law about it, and tried your best to impoverish us, and then offered to buy our house — O, O! And your little boys have learned to call us names, and to fling stones at *me!* Say, was that wicked?" And Mr. Grash's Cat bounced up and down in a rage, with both paws stretched out.

"You shall have a piece of my mind, neighbor," said Mr. Frome's Cat, getting up in great excitement and standing on the very edge of the slippery roof. "But, O dear!" he said, as his feet sank in the cold snow, "here we are quarreling again over this old matter," and he returned to his shelter by the window. "Do, pray, let us leave this horrid subject. What a charming night!"

Mr. Frome's Cat meant well, but he did not have much tact.

"A charming night!" hissed the other. "Say, what is the piece of your mind? O, how grand you feel!"

"You're hungry, friend," said Mr. Frome's Cat, soothingly. "Come, let us see what we can find."

"And well I may be," retorted the other fiercely, "with your high wall — O!"

"Well," said his neighbor, eager to keep the peace, "just jump across, and we'll go down there."

Now Mr. Grash's Cat never had jumped across before, but the temptation was so great to the hungry fellow that he did not hesitate more than a moment, and made the leap. Alas! perhaps he was weak, perhaps the distance was more than he thought, — poor Mr. Grash's Cat just jumped into the air and went down, down, over and over, to the ground between the two houses. Mr. Frome's Cat saw him disappear; Mr. Frome's Cat rushed to the edge to look after his comrade; the roof was steep, the snow slipped, and Mr. Frome's Cat went down, down, over and over, to the ground; both were in the air at once, but of course Mr. Grash's Cat reached bottom first, and each as they fell uttered a long scream.

At the sound, a window in Mr. Grash's house opening upon the place, was thrown up, and a head appeared.

" O dear! " said a nervous voice, " O dear! " and the head peering down, discovered the two cats, who were now sitting together, rubbing their heads to collect their wits. " Scat! " said the voice; " Shu, shu! " and round the corner darted the two bewildered cats, leaping the iron picket fence.

The next morning was Christmas. The snow lay heavily on the ground, but it had stopped falling, and the sky was clear; the air was sparkling with freshness, and it was a real pleasure to be in it, to draw it into the warm lungs, and send it out again in whiffs of vapor. A little boy was shoveling snow in front of Mr. Frome's house, and he seemed like a miniature steam-engine, puffing at his work, and pitching the snow into the street with regular tosses, while every now and then he would stop, as if the fireman to the engine had opened a valve, and was to let off a little more steam first. This was Tommy Frome, who was clearing the sidewalk in front of his father's house, while his little brother and sister watched him from behind the window of the dining-room, where they were waiting for breakfast. Jack, who had begged hard to go out and shovel snow, was kept in with a great cold in his head, so that he was snuffing disagreeably, and had his handkerchief in a hard round ball. Sally was perfectly well, and was playing with one of her Christmas presents, — a Nuremberg India-rubber man, whose head, being shoved down into his stomach, would very slowly rise, as the air filled him from a little hole behind, until it bobbed up, uttered a little squeak, shook itself with another squeak, and then held itself erect, with an anxious and injured expression on the face. Sally kept knocking on the window for Tommy to see it, but he could not hear it squeak, and so it did not seem so droll to him.

At last the little steam-engine outside had finished the work, and was coming into the house with a great deal of stamping; and kicking off his India - rubber boots, Tommy Frome entered the dining-room, blowing great blasts on his nose, which was as red as his ears and his cheeks. His father and mother were there by the fire, and breakfast was ready, to which they all sat down.

"Well, Tommy," said Mr. Frome, "did you clear all the snow off?"

"Yes, sir-r-r," said Tommy, who was in high spirits, "all on our sidewalk; but there isn't much gone off Old Grash's sidewalk — not much. I let him have some of ours."

> "Grash-away! Grash-away! let hib alode!
> He lives with his wife, add his cat, add a bode,"

sung Master Jack, as well as he could, with his organ out of tune.

"Jack!" said his mother.

"That's what all the boys sing, mother," said Sally, "and Old Grash shakes his stick at them. What makes them call him Grash-away?"

"Because he's so cross," said Tom; "and he had no business to build his house where he did — had he, father?"

"Do," said Jack; "add I bead to burd it dowd sub dight."

"I guess that will burn ours pretty quick, youngster," said his older brother.

"Well, we could build ours again," said Sally, "but he isn't rich enough to build his."

"Children," said their mother, glancing at Mr. Frome, "who wants to go to Aunt Martha's to-day?"

"Me!" said three bad grammarians in one voice. So they fell to talking about Aunt Martha the rest of breakfast time, but Mr. Frome said little. He felt uncomfortably; and, when breakfast was over, he pushed his chair away and sat by the fire, while the children played and talked together. He was uneasy. Here were his children growing up and catching at his dislike of his neighbor; keeping the quarrel alive, and shooting, perhaps every day, little irritating arrows of words at Mr. Grash, which he himself would have been ashamed, of course, to use. But yet, did he not have in his heart the hard, cross feelings toward his neighbor which his children put into words, while they had no special grudge, but only caught their father's dislike?

"Hush, children; we are going to have prayers now," said Mrs. Frome, and she handed the family Bible to her husband. He took it, open at the place which she had found, and still thinking of his neighbor, himself, and his children, he read the story of the birth of the Lord Jesus, of the angel that came to the shepherds, with his wonderful words: "Unto you is born this day, in the city of David, a Saviour, which is Christ the Lord. And this shall be a sign unto you: ye shall find the babe wrapped in swaddling-clothes, lying in a manger." And then, how the multitude of the heavenly host burst into their song of praise, perhaps at the very moment when, leaning eagerly out of heaven, they saw the Babe born upon earth. O divine song, that never since has died away! for always there are new voices to take it up, in heaven and on earth, none singing out of tune, — but poor, feeble, cracked voices of earthly singers chiming in with the full notes of angels. Mr. Frome read the words, too, that Christmas morning, and then, as was their wont, the family kneeled in prayer. Mr. Frome's lips uttered some words, he scarcely knew what: they were but sounds, for his heart was wandering away, thinking of those joyful words, and what a life of sorrow and suffering they ushered in. "Yes," he murmured in his prayer, "God so loved the world;" and he thought within himself that it was when God gave up His son that He bade the joyful choir of angels sing. His voice trembled; he fell into the Lord's Prayer, in which the rest joined, and only when he uttered the words, "Forgive us our debts as we forgive our debtors," did poor Mr. Frome's mind come back and throw itself fervently into his words.

"Mother," he said hastily, as he rose, "I am going in to see neighbor Grash. Tommy, just bring me my boots, will you?"

"And do ask how Mrs. Grash is, John," said Mrs. Frome, looking very much pleased. "I saw the doctor's chaise at the door yesterday, and I am afraid she is sick. I would have sent to inquire, but" — and she looked a little shyly at her husband.

"Ahem!" said he, getting something out of his throat, "you are right, you are always right, Mary; it was wrong, it is all wrong; I begin to see it," and ejaculating such short sentences as he tugged at his boots, Mr. Frome grew red in the face, and, kissing his wife, went into the entry. He came back in a moment. "Tom," said he, "can you act like a little gentleman? I want you to come with me and see Mr. Grash."

"O bah!" said the boy.

"I'd go, Tobby," said Jack. "Ask hib how his cat is."

"Jack," said his mother, quietly, "Mr. Grash hasn't any rude little boys to call us names."

Tom hung back a minute more, and then, seeing his father waiting, he ran out and pulled his boots up over his feet, and his tippet down over his head, and so was ready, nodding back to the rest in the window, as he and his father went down the steps and on to the sidewalk. At that moment the door of their neighbor's house opened, and Mr. Grash stepped out into the street. Mr. Frome was flustered a moment. He had expected to ring the door-bell, and he had not collected his thoughts yet.

"Eh! ah!" said he; "O, Mr. Grash, a merry Christmas to you — I wish you a merry Christmas!" and he pulled at his glove, and thrust his hand out with the glove flapping at the tip, for he could not get it off before Mr. Grash had held out his hand in its mitten, and had shaken it up and down a great many times.

"Yes, indeed, a merry Christmas, Mr. Frome — at least I hope so. Doing pretty well. I say, do you think your wife? — You know — the doctor said he'd come again — he hasn't come yet — do you see him?" and Mr. Grash looked anxiously down the street.

"Why, what — O! ah! Tommy, run into the house at once, and tell your mother to come quick — just as quick as she can — to Mr.

Grash's. Tell her Mrs. Grash has a little boy. Mr. Grash, I wish you joy, most heartily."

"Why, didn't you know it?" asked Mr. Grash, looking amazed.

"I ought to have known it, being your nearest neighbor, Grash, but really — I — I was coming to wish you a merry Christmas," said Mr. Frome, turning a little redder, "and I thought it would not be merry to me unless I wiped out old scores."

"Well, now," said Mr. Grash, "I'm glad to hear you say so, for last night, as I was watching and waiting, I turned it all over, and I made up my mind that the first thing I'd do this morning would be to go to you, and — and — take it all back. Mr. Frome," he went on, after a moment, "it was my wife's doing. She said to me last night — says she, 'If I die, Simon, you'll make it all up with Mr. Frome — won't you? You know we were the wrong ones.' As if she was wrong, Mr. Frome! Somehow, I can't feel this morning as I did yesterday — or day before yesterday, I mean. This sitting up all night confuses one so. I want to be at peace with everybody. I feel as if some one had been ringing bells or singing songs."

At this moment back came Tommy with his

mother, and by her was little Sally. Poor Jack stood behind the window, his ball of a handkerchief up at his face, now blowing his nose and now wiping his tears, because he couldn't go over and see Mr. Grash's baby, but must stay in the house for fear of catching more cold. Mrs. Frome shook hands warmly with Mr. Grash, and little Sally came boldly up and said, —

"Merry Christmas, Mr. Grash! Mother says I can't see the baby, but here is something I'll lend her. I can't give it, you know, because it was a present to me this morning. You must do *so;*" and so saying, Sally held up the Nuremberg India-rubber man, and shoved his head into his stomach, and then gravely watched Mr. Grash to see what he would do when the head popped up. Mr. Grash laughed louder than any one had laughed yet, and she was perfectly satisfied.

"There!" said she, triumphantly, "give that to her! give that to the baby. I mean, show it to her," for as Mr. Grash took it, Sally had a sudden fear she might never see it again.

"I'll send it back by your mother," said he; "but it is a little boy-baby, my little girl."

"O, I thought it was a girl," said Sally, a little bit disappointed. "Well, never mind," she spoke up quite cheerfully; "I've got two brothers, and they're both boys."

"Mr. Grash," said Tommy, "I'd like to clean off your walk. I like shoveling snow."

"There's a little man!" said Mr. Grash, who was finding it quite hard to get back into his house again, what with his new friends and their offers of neighborliness. So the door shut behind Mr. Grash and his neighbor Mr. Frome, and his neighbor's wife; and the two children remained outside, Tommy shoveling snow, and Sally watching him, while Jacky, whose tears were dried, was now rubbing his thumb up the window-pane, and making what was music to him.

At the back of Mr. Frome's house was a high wall, shutting in the yard. A gate opened in it, but it was closed, and by it outside sat two cats. They were Mr. Frome's Cat and Mr. Grash's Cat.

"Perhaps, if we scratch a little harder, she might come," said Mr. Grash's Cat, looking wistfully at the gate.

"My claws are rather tender," said Mr. Frome's Cat; "I think I could mew better. I wish the wall were not so high."

"Don't speak of the high wall, my dear

friend, said Mr. Grash's Cat. "You make me feel so ashamed of myself. To think that I should ever" —

"Not another word," said Mr. Frome's Cat, raising his paw playfully. "A high wall shall not separate us, who are neighbors. Hark!" At that moment the cook opened the gate, and both cats at once ran in. The gate was shut after them, and so nothing more could be seen. But something was heard. It was a sort of scraping sound on a tin pan.

## GOOD AND BAD APPLES.

THERE was a little apple-tree near the garden wall, which was called Rob's apple-tree, because it was set out on the very day when he was five years old, and he himself with his own little spade helped fill in the earth round the roots, and stamped it down, while Quick, his dog, barked at him.

"You needn't laugh, Quick," said he, "for I am to have all the apples that grow on this tree;" and then he ran off to quarrel with Quick, for they both liked that exceedingly. Not far from the tree was the plaster statue of a young man leaning on a hoe, — Old Hoe, as Rob called him, — though he was not so very old, and yet he leaned with such a wise air, and looked abroad so seriously, that it was generally said in the garden, — It is Old Hoe who has scraped up the earth — everything grows because he made the ground ready — and now he has nothing to do but to watch the trees and flowers, and think about them;" and when Rob and Quick and the gardener were gone, Old Hoe thought aloud as usual: —

"So, here is a new-comer, and it is to bear apples — is it? It has a very serious task before it. It takes a great deal to make an apple. It must rain just so often, and the sun must shine just so many days, and the wind must not blow too hard, and it must not hail when the blossoms come. It is a wonder that there are ever any apples at all; and then, they are picked and put in a basket. Seems to me it is hardly worth while to go through so many troubles, just to be picked and put in a basket."

"But what am I to do?" asked the young apple-tree. Old Hoe did not answer; he never was known to join in talk with others. The world might hear, if it liked, when he spoke out, but he had too many thoughts in his head to allow him merely to make conversation. The sun shone, the rain fell, the wind blew, there was hail and snow and ice, and by and by six blossoms came upon the little apple-tree; and after the blossoms came just two apples, for the other four blossoms came to nothing. Two rosy apples! the little tree was very proud of them.

"Ah! two apples," said Old Hoe one day;

"they are not very large either. Seems to me it is rather a small affair for the wind, and the sun, and the rain, and this apple-tree, to work so hard and only make two apples. Why should not everything make everything bigger than itself?" and Old Hoe stared down the garden. A hen just then laid an egg under the hedge, and was off telling her neighbors. "Now that hen made an egg," Old Hoe went on; "but seems to me the egg ought to have made the hen." He was puzzled, but nobody would suspect it, for he looked very grave. The little apple-tree, meanwhile, was lifting up her head bravely, and holding out her two apples at arm's length, on opposite sides, so that they could not well see each other. They could talk, however, though they had not much to say. They were twins.

"Brother," said One to the Other, "how do you grow to-day? Do you feel pretty mellow?"

"I can't yet feel very warm," said the Other, "but then the sun is not very high. How delightful it is to be getting riper every day. I only hope we shall not be picked too soon. I should like to be perfectly ripe first."

"Well, brother," said One, with hesitation, "I — I do not perfectly agree with you. I begin to think that we have made a little mistake, and that there is something besides getting ripe and being picked and put in a basket. In fact," said he, speaking more confidently, "I know that there is something better, for I am already beginning to enjoy it."

"Why, how can that be?" asked the Other. "We get the sun and the air and the sap, and so we grow warm and ripe. Come! is there anything better? what is your secret?"

"It is not easily told," said One, mysteriously, "but you shall hear something. Yesterday afternoon, as I was beginning to dread the night, I heard something on the twig, and pretty soon felt it on my stem; it came slowly down until it was firmly on me. 'Who may you be?' said I, a little angrily, I must confess. 'Do not be disturbed, good sir,' said a soft voice; 'I am a friend come to visit you. You will be the better for me, I assure you. I am Tid, the worm.' I had never heard of him before, but he was so soft and comfortable in his ways, that I knew he was a friend at once, and so I welcomed him. 'It is lonely enough here,' said I, 'for my brother never can come to see me, and my only amusement is when the wind blows, and I get a chance to rock back and forth, and that is sometimes a little too hard.' 'Just so,' said Tid. 'I have been waiting for you some time on the grass below, hoping some windy day you might fall off and come to see me, for it is very hard work climbing so high. I have waited long enough, and now I am here, glad to get to my journey's end.' At that, Tid stood on his head, I thought. 'What are you doing, Tid?' said I. 'I am going,' said he, 'to bring you a new pleasure. Have a care; don't joggle me off.' Brother, those were his exact words."

"Well," said the Other, "and what is the new pleasure. Is it to walk round on you and keep you warm?"

"Better than that," said One. "Do you know, if you could look round here, you would n't see Tid?"

"Not see him! has he gone then?"

"Yes, yes," said One, bursting out with it; "he has gone in! he has gone in!"

"Gone in!"

"You know I told you I thought Tid was standing on his head; so he was; and he began to make a little hole in me, not far from the stem, and put his head in, and so, deeper and deeper, till now, my dear brother, Tid is entirely inside!"

"Well," said the Other, "do you call that pleasant?"

"Pleasant!" cried One. "Growing ripe is nothing to it. Why, there is Tid, comfortable little soul, burrowing and burrowing, and the further in he goes, the easier it is for the sun to get inside, you know; but the warmth is not the great pleasure; it's the tickling! the tickling! Tid is tickling me all the time, and I sit here and laugh."

"Dear me!" said the Other, "and Tid is doing all this for you; and how does he like it?"

"There! I just hear him talking to himself. Hark!"

"Well, what does Tid say?" asked the Other.

"He says, — 'Munch, munch! I must be getting toward the core. I have not had such a feast this long while. I came just at the right time. The apple and I will get ripe together. I shall go on, too, after picking-time comes.' There! do you hear that? You see Tid and I are not going to stop when I get ripe."

"I don't know about this," said the Other. "Why, Tid 's hollowing you out — isn't he? and suppose he leaves nothing but your skin?"

"All I know is," said One sharply, "that I get a new delight all the while, and don't put off my pleasure till I am picked and put in a basket." The Other was silent, but he kept thinking, and the more he thought, the more sure he was that he should not wish a visit from Tid. That went on for several days, and they agreed less and less whenever they fell to talking.

"Halloo!" cried One, one day, "what do you think? I am getting popular. Tid's friends missed him, and now they have come — three more, uncommonly like Tid. They have all gone in, too, and each by different holes."

"I must speak out," said the Other. "I am certain that it is all wrong, and I do beseech you, brother, to get rid of Tid and his relations. There is no time to lose."

"Indeed!" said One. "I understand you perfectly; if, now, Tid had visited you — but we will say no more;" and so for several days nothing more was said; nothing by them, that is, for Old Hoe at length spoke out: —

"Seems to me strange that those apples do not do anything to get ripe. They just hang and hang. I could hang, but should I be the better for that? Seems to me if they were to get down and roll round on the ground, they would be doing something, — would be getting on with their ripening. There is the gardener; if he were to stand still all day, would the garden take care of itself?"

The gardener was at this moment coming up toward the tree; perhaps the twins saw him; at any rate One called out with a faint voice, —

"Brother, a word with you. I feel exceedingly weak."

"Cheer up, cheer up!" said the Other. "We must be quite ripe now; we shall soon be picked and put in a basket."

"Ah! you are very well; but as for me, I must confess it, I have been growing weaker every day. Tid and his relations have been all through me, and I cannot tell why, but I feel very disagreeably. Somehow all the pleasure is gone, and I have headache perpetually." Just here the gardener came up to the tree, and Rob and Quick came running to him from the other side of the garden.

"Daniel, are they ripe, do you think? May I pick them?" asked Rob.

"Well, Master Rob," said he, "you'll not get two; one is all worm-eaten, but t'other is a rosy, ripe apple." He picked them both and tossed one away, but the other he gave to Rob. Quick darted after the apple that was thrown away; he snuffed at it, but let it alone.

"Here, here, Quick!" said Rob: "That is a bad apple. This is a good one," and he ran off, holding it up, while Quick bounded after him. The gardener, too, went off, and no one was left but Old Hoe.

"This is the end — eh?" said he. "One is thrown away and the other is picked; it should have been put in a basket. It is pretty hard to have so much trouble, and then not get all one's deserts. Why was it not put in a basket?" The apple thrown away had rolled quite near Old Hoe, and he now saw it. "So this was a bad apple! Why, what had it done? it had all the rain and sun like the other, and it was picked. It was not put in a basket, but neither was the other. I don't understand."

"I understand," said the apple. "If I had joggled Tid off when he first came, as I might have done, all would have been well, but now it is all over. O dear, they are all going about again! and I have such a headache." In a few moments Tid and his relations had put their heads out of their several doors.

"What's this?" said Tid. "We were all living peaceably. What have you been doing to shake us about so? I nearly had a fit. Aha! I see; friends, we are on the ground once more. Come, I like this. I was beginning to dread climbing down the tree, and there's not much left here. But we'll finish what we have begun," and, so saying, all crawled in again.

Old Hoe heard this also, but was too astonished to do anything but lean on his instrument and stare off into the garden. Perhaps he would have been more puzzled if he could have followed Rob with his apple. Rob ran into the house, and fetching a string from his pocket, he tied one end to the stem of the apple, and so hung it over the fire, twirling it round and round. The apple was a little dizzy at first, but in a moment was perfectly delighted at such a dance as he led; the pleasure he had felt when the wind blew him was nothing to this. Then the heat of the fire began to warm him and to creep deliciously through and through; why, the brightest sunshine had never so made him glow. The little apple laughed and shook with merriment; he could not keep in, and actually burst his sides out with joy, all the while humming a tune, being the first time he had ever sung in his life, and this was the song that Little Apple sung: —

"All summer long
I sang no song
Upon the green-leaved tree:
But let the sun
Sing, one by one,
The summer songs to me.

"The songs I hid
  My seeds amid,
Until they eager grew:
  My lips, alas!
  They could not pass,
To sing themselves anew.

"Then bright flames leapt
  To where I kept
My pretty songs in cage:
  They burst the bars
  With glad ha, ha's!
And mocked at my old age.

"Out flew the songs,
  The summer songs;
And now they sing to me
  The joys I knew
  All summer through,
Upon the apple-tree."

## THREE WISE LITTLE BOYS.

Christmas always falls on the twenty-fifth of December, even if it is leap year, which joggles the almanac so, and sometimes the twenty-fifth is Sunday; and so it happened one year that in the little village of Blessington, Christmas and Sunday and the twenty-fifth of December all fell on the same day; and more than that, little Jacob Olds's birthday was on the same day; and when I tell you that little Jacob was exactly, to a day, one year younger than his brothers John and Peter Olds, you will see what a great occasion it was when the twenty-fifth of December, and Christmas, and Sunday, and little Jacob's birthday, and John's birthday, and Peter's birthday, all happened together: and O, one thing more — Mr. and Mrs. Olds were married on Christmas eight years before, and this was leap year. I suppose it is not very often that such a Christmas happens.

The evening before this Christmas, John

and Peter and little Jacob were playing about their father and mother just before bed-time. The pretty room was nicely furnished, for there was Mr. Olds with his newspaper, pretending to read, and Mrs. Olds with her sewing, pretending to sew, and Peter and John and little Jacob playing about like three little kittens. Little Jacob finally climbed into his father's lap and pretended to read the newspaper too. There was a long column of print all about the financial difficulties of Austria, and Jaky read it aloud to his father somewhat thus, with his fat finger moving over the lines: —

"On Christmas morning children have presents from their papas and mammas. Sometimes they are in stockings, but ours are on a big table. Some boys like books, but I like a sled. I think my papa will give me a sled," — here he had nearly reached the bottom of the column, he read so fast, and so he ended up, — "and we wish you all a merry Christmas. Yours truly, Jacob Olds and Company."

"O, is that in the newspaper?" asked Peter, who had been listening. "Why, that's my father's name."

"Pooh, you goose," said John, who was exactly of the same age, but always treated Peter as if he were years younger, "that's Jaky. He made it up."

" O," said Peter, who was not very quick, "I thought he was reading. Mamma, what is Christmas, any way? It isn't Sunday, is it?"

"I know," said John. "It's the day when presents are given. You have to say 'Merry Christmas' to everybody, and the one who gets up first and says it, is the best fellow."

"Then I'll get up first," said Peter. "You wake me, will you, mamma?"

"Hoh," said John, "you're great. If mother wakes up first she'll say it."

"Any way," said Peter, "we're going to have a great dinner. I heard Becky say so, and she says folks always have a great dinner on Christmas."

"Becky knows ever so much," said little Jacob. She knows a lot she won't tell. She knows something about Christmas that's a secret, I guess. I said Christmas was my birthday" —

"It's my birthday too," said Peter, who wanted to have everything that anybody else had.

"Well, it's mine, too," said John. "Anybody'd think you owned it. Does Christmas always come on Sunday, father? To-morrow 's Sunday."

"It hasn't anything to do with Sunday," said Mr. Olds. "It only happens so."

"Becky says," went on Jacob, "that she's always glad when Christmas comes on Sunday, and when I asked her why, she said because somebody she knew about was born on Christmas, and liked Sunday. I don't think that's much."

At this moment Becky herself, the old nurse, appeared in the doorway to lead the children to bed. They went frolicking upstairs, and Mr. and Mrs. Olds were left alone. Mrs. Olds stitched on in silence for a moment, and then looked timidly at her husband, who sat behind the newspaper.

"My heart misgives me, Jacob," said she. "I don't know, I sometimes think it would be better if the children were to know — to know something about what people generally know — what they read in the Bible."

"Becky hasn't been telling them any stories out of the Bible, has she?" asked Mr. Olds, impatiently. "I told her when she came, that if I ever found her telling religious stuff to my children, she should leave at once. I'm not going to have her putting nonsense into their heads. I intend they shall grow up rationally, and make up their minds for themselves, without any prejudice."

"I don't think she has," said his wife, with a doubtful look on her face. "You see how she checked herself when Jaky asked her about Christmas. She feels pretty badly, though, about it."

"Let her," said Mr. Olds, pushing his spectacles hard down on his nose. "It's not her concern, at least."

Becky had taken the three children to the room in which they all slept in their little beds, and had tucked them in, and then, as was her wont, had got down upon her poor old knees and prayed hastily within herself that the Lord would bless the darlings, and send somebody to teach them; while the children, as usual, kept still, because Becky was looking under the beds, as they thought, to see if anybody was there, and their little hearts were always in a little fright till Becky got up again and kissed them, and told them that they might go to sleep, for somebody was watching over them, and would keep them safe; and as they always found Becky there when they woke up, they had no doubt she was the Somebody, and Peter when he heard Becky say somebody was watching over them, secretly thought that Becky herself climbed up on the bed-post and sat there all night, where she could see them all, and could keep off danger.

But this night the children were wide awake, and begged Becky to stay and tell them a story, or sing a song. The poor old thing had her head full of Bible stories and hymns, but she had been forbidden to tell them to the children, and so she had to fall back on the days of her childhood, when she lived in a little village of England.

"Tell us what you used to do when you were a little girl," said John.

"Sing us a song," said Peter.

"I know," said little Jacob; "tell us about Christmas, Becky. Tell us about the man that had his birthday then, and liked Sunday. You know" —

"Who was it?" asked Peter.

"It was somebody," began poor Becky, at her wit's end how to tell what she longed to tell, without disobeying, and so making a sad mystery of it all.

"O, was it Somebody," cried Peter, "Somebody who watches over us? But you're a woman, Becky."

"The dear child," said the puzzled old body, "so I am. If I was only a man, like old Parson Dawes that used to be" —

"Tell us about Parson Dawes," struck in John, who thought they were not getting on with a story.

"Well, I will," said old Becky, suddenly brightening up, "and I'll just tell you about what Parson Dawes did when I was a little girl. Parson Dawes he was a good man, a very good man, but he hadn't no children of his own, and so says he one Christmas time to the chorister, — that's my father, children" —

"O Becky, you're making up," said Peter; "you haven't got any father."

"But I had one, Peter, when I was a little girl."

"Was it Somebody?" asked John, who thought that Becky was always making believe when she spoke of Somebody.

"The dear children," murmured the old woman. "Says he, says Parson Dawes to my father, 'Simon,' he says, 'they used to have a custom for children to go about Christmas Eve and sing carols. Now, you just teach the children to sing one, and I'll go round with the children myself and sing it.' He was a nice old man, Parson Dawes, but folks thought he was rather queer, p'raps because he didn't have no children of his own. So my father, he taught us children a carol which Parson Dawes he gave him; and sure enough we went round, and Parson Dawes he went with us, and we sang, and we sang — O, it was beautiful," and nurse Becky, forgetting everything except what she was remembering, and forgetting her own poor cracked old voice, piped out to a sweet air the words:—

"'God rest you, merry gentlemen,
Let nothing you dismay,
For Jesus Christ, our Saviour,
Was born upon this day,
To save us all from Satan's power,
When we were gone astray.

"'In Bethlehem, in Jewry,
This blessed babe was born,
And laid within a manger
Upon this blessed morn;
The which his mother, Mary,
Nothing did take in scorn.

"'From God, our Heavenly Father,
A blessed angel came,
And unto certain shepherds
Brought tidings of the same,
How that in Bethlehem was born
The Son of God by name.

"'Fear not, then said the angel,
Let nothing you affright,
This day is born a Saviour
Of virtue, power, and might;
So frequently to vanquish all
The friends of Satan quite.

"'The shepherds at those tidings
Rejoicéd much in mind,

And left their flocks a-feeding
  In tempest, storm, and wind,
And went to Bethlehem straightway,
  This blessed babe to find.

"'But when to Bethlehem they came,
  Whereas this infant lay,
They found Him in a manger,
  Where oxen feed on hay,
His mother Mary kneeling,
  Unto the Lord did pray.

"'Now to the Lord sing praise,
  All you within this place,
And with true love and brotherhood,
  Each other now embrace;
This holy tide of Christmas
  All others doth deface.
    O tidings of comfort and joy!
    For Jesus Christ our Saviour
    Was born on Christmas Day.'"

"And did Parson Dawes sing it all with the children?" asked John.

"Indeed he did," said Becky, warming with the recollection. "We just went from one house to another a-singing, and Parson Dawes he carried a stick and pounded on the ground when we sang. He was just daft-like, when we was a-singing, and he took to his bed that very night, and so he died."

This was quite unexpected, and Peter began to cry.

"What made him die?" said he, whimpering. "What made Parson Dawes die? I didn't want him to die."

Little Jacob had said nothing, but his busy little head was trying to put together what nurse had said and sung.

"Nurse," said he, "do please sing that again. That part about the shepherds."

So Becky sang again: —

"'The shepherds at those tidings
Rejoicéd much in mind,
And left their flocks a-feeding
In tempest, storm, and wind,
And went to Bethlehem straightway,
This blessed babe to find.
O tidings of comfort and joy!
For Jesus Christ our Saviour
Was born on Christmas Day.

"'But when to Bethlehem they came,
Whereas this infant lay,
They found him in a manger,
Where oxen feed on hay,
His mother Mary kneeling,
Unto the Lord did pray.'"

"But what made them go to Bethlem?" asked John. "What's Bethlem?"

"Why, it's where the babe was," said little Jacob. "Don't you see?"

"The little babe that was born, was Jesus

Christ the Lord," said old Becky reverently, clasping her hands and lifting up her face. "And He was the Lord of glory who had come down on earth to live, and He was born a little babe in a manger, and when the shepherds they came, they found the little babe a-lying in the manger; and the little babe grew up, and He healed the sick, and He taught us about God and heaven, and then wicked men killed Him, and then He died for us — poor little children," — broke out old Becky, choking down her sobs; "and I wasn't to tell you, but I couldn't help it if I was to leave this night — there!" And the old nurse threw herself down on her knees, and wept and prayed aloud that the good Lord would teach the little ignorant ones, and tell them about Jesus when Becky left.

"O, don't go," said Jaky, "don't go, nurse. We don't want 'Good Lord;' we want you. I'm going to sing that over again," and he tried to sing the verse that had been sung last. He came pretty near it, and the other children took hold with great eagerness, and insisted on singing it too. They had sweet voices, and pretty soon old Becky with her cracked voice, and the three children, were all singing together.

But Becky began to be troubled, and said she must not stay any longer, and that the children must go to sleep. So she kissed them once more and went out softly. The children could not go to sleep, they were so excited.

"It was a secret," said John. "She said she wasn't to tell. I guess father and mother were keeping it for a surprise."

"I guess it was Somebody that was born," said Peter. "And then He died, just like Parson Dawes."

"I wish we could have heard them all sing," said little Jacob; "it must have sounded like what the shepherds heard."

"I say," said John, in a hurried whisper. "Let's us."

"What?" said little Jacob, starting up.

"Let's us sing," said John.

"Well," said Peter, beginning, —

"'The shepherds at those tidings'" —

"No, no," said John, impatiently. "Peter, Peter, I don't mean here, but let's play we were Parson Dawes and the children. I'll be Parson Dawes and you be the children, and we'll sing, just as they did."

"O do," said little Jacob eagerly, and he bounced out of bed. "Johnny, Johnny, we'll put on our things and go out, and nobody will hear us, and then we'll sing."

So the three children dressed hurriedly in the dark, Peter much wondering in his puzzled head whether John, when he got through, was going to take to his bed and die, like Parson Dawes. They groped about, talking to each other in loud whispers, and putting on their clothes in all sorts of new ways. At last all were dressed, except that Peter could not lace his shoe, so he let the lacing go dragging after him.

"We can't get our hats," said John. "I tell you what. We'll take blankets."

So each of the children took a blanket off the bed and wrapped it round himself and over his head, and so with suppressed giggles the three little blanketed figures stole down-stairs and out-of-doors. There was no snow on the hard ground; there was no moonlight either, but the bright stars were shining as they stepped forth, shutting the door noiselessly behind them.

"Parson Dawes had a stick," said Peter, "and he pounded with it when the children sang. You haven't got any stick, John."

"Yes, I have," said he triumphantly, showing a hearth-broom which he had concealed under his blanket. "I thought of it. I'm Parson Dawes. Now, children, when I begin to pound, we must all sing."

They were standing under the window of the room where they had bade their father and mother good-night. The curtain was dropped, but a bright light was behind it. In vain, however, the children sang, and Parson Dawes pounded. No one came to the window.

"Papa! mamma!" shouted Peter. "See us! we're Parson Dawes and the children."

"Sh!" said little Jacob. "That isn't the way. Let's go to Mr. Lirry's."

Mr. Lirry lived next door, and again did Parson Dawes and his choir sing and pound in vain. They tried the next street. A wagon drove by, and the man in it stopped and turned to look at the three queer little figures.

"I'm afraid," said Peter, beginning to run down a side street. John and little Jacob were not afraid, but they ran after him, and the man in the wagon drove off in another direction, but they thought he was chasing them, so they all ran in good earnest; but the noise of the wheels died away, and they came to a halt by a stone wall.

"O Peter, what made you run?" said John, all out of breath.

"Where are we?" said Peter. But it was so dark, and they had got so bewildered with the run, that the poor little things could not tell.

"We must turn round and go back," said John, clinging to his hearth-brush, and determined, like a brave little fellow, that he would defend them. They began to sing again, and somehow the stars shone so brightly, and the music sounded so sweetly, that they walked along without fear, and even Peter began to chatter about many things.

"This is just the night," said little Jacob, "to find a babe in. I shouldn't wonder, no, I shouldn't wonder one bit, if we were to see some shepherds, and should find a barn, and there in the manger would be a babe. Only think of it. Wouldn't Becky be glad?"

"She said there was a star over it," said Peter, "a bright star, and it was right over the place. I don't see where we are, and I'm cold."

"I see a barn," said little Jacob. "Yes, I see it plainly, and O! what a bright star; and it is growing brighter too."

And indeed just at that moment it did seem as if a particularly bright star shone above the barn. The children were all alive with eagerness as they came up to it.

"What if we should go right in and find him there!" said little Jacob, his eyes starting out of his head. "Johnny, we must sing the song."

Then they stood by the barn and sang the verses, Peter holding on to little Jacob, and John striking the ground with his stick like Parson Dawes. They lifted the latch of the door and peered in. It was darker in there than out, but it was warmer, and so, creeping in, they closed the door after them. Peter clung close to little Jacob, and now as they stood there, their little hearts beating, a light began to fill the place gently, and their eyes becoming accustomed to the darkness, they began to make out things. There stood some oxen, and there too were some sheep, all lying in their pens and stalls. The light that came was the rising moon, which rose higher and higher, sending its light through a great easterly window. The children crept up to a manger, and peered eagerly and yet timidly over.

"Perhaps he has not come yet," said John. "Let's wait."

There was a hay-cart standing on the barn-floor half filled with hay, and into this the three little children clambered and lay close together, waiting till the Child should appear.

It was about the time that the three children were clambering up into the hay-cart that Mr. and Mrs. Olds, who had been taking little naps

all the evening, thought it as well to go to bed once for all. Mrs. Olds indeed had felt that she would gladly go and sleep off the uncomfortable thoughts that began to visit her.

"Jacob," said she, "it was eight Christmases ago that we were married."

"Well, Rachel," said he, good-humoredly, as he took off his spectacles, "I expect you will give us a first-rate dinner in honor of the day."

"Yes, and it's the children's birthday, too, and Christmas. I wonder what sort of a notion they have of Christmas?"

"A very correct notion," said Mr. Olds, restlessly, — "a day of frolic, of giving and receiving presents, and eating plum-pudding. They shall have a merry Christmas."

"Won't they come to ask why it all happened on Christmas-day?" continued the mother, thoughtfully.

"Well, wife, they'll learn it all by and by, when they study history; and they won't have any nonsensical notions about it."

At this moment Annie, the maid, came to say that Becky, the nurse, would like to speak to the master and mistress, if she might, and right behind came Becky, with her eyes very red, and her hands twitching at her dress.

"Come in, Becky; what is it?" said Mrs. Olds.

"Please, ma'am, I must a-go."

"Why, don't we treat you well?" asked Mr. Olds in surprise.

"O Mr. Olds — I could'nt help it, ma'am; but when those darling children asked me about Christmas, and I got to telling them about the hymn which we children used to sing with Parson Dawes when I was a little girl, I couldn't help it, sir; but O, I told them about the Babe that lay in the manger, and how the shepherds heard the angels sing, and the Wise Men of the East, how they came and brought presents; and O, Mrs. Olds, I couldn't a-bear that the darling children shouldn't hear about the blessed Jesus, who said, 'Suffer little children to come unto me,' and you don't let them go; and I thought, says I, if the Lord asks me, Becky, why didn't you let them come? what made you a-hinder them, — and so I told them, and now I'll go, sir, as I heard you said I must;" and the poor old woman, who had rushed through her words which she had been all the evening making up her mind to say, quite broke down, and sobbed into the lap of her great gown.

Mr. Olds walked up and down the room uneasily, and Mrs. Olds, half ready to cry and half ready to be downright angry with Becky, stood still by the fire.

"I'll see you in the morning," said Mr. Olds, giving his coat a twist, and buttoning it about him, and then, as Becky left, he turned to his wife, —

"Come, Rachel, we'll go to bed; but first we'll look in on the children, to make sure they haven't been spirited away by some of Becky's invisible friends," adding a worried little laugh. They took their light and went up-stairs. They entered the room.

"Merciful Heavens!" cried Mrs. Olds, and Mr. Olds roared, —

"Becky!"

The whole house was roused and in a tumult. The servants crowded into the room, and a great wailing was made. Mr. Olds, raising his voice above the din, while his wife was dumb and white, ordered quiet, and striking Becky on the shoulder and holding her at arm's length away, he bade her tell him where the children were.

"Please God," said the old woman, "I left them lying awake in their beds, and I have not been in the room since."

"She's been in her room crying like everything the whole evening," spoke up Annie, the maid. There was silence a moment, and then Mr. Olds said, —

"None of you leave the house."

It was hardly necessary to say this; not one scarcely dared to leave the room, but Becky said meekly, —

"Please, master, I must go. I must find the children."

Mr. Olds said nothing, but went out of the room with his wife. He put on his coat, and she mechanically dressed herself, and together they went out of the house, but not alone, for Becky had followed, bearing a lantern in her hand. They went from one house to another, and the neighbors joined them in the search, till the whole village was astir.

"Neighbor," said Mr. Lirry, "about what time was it you might have missed your children?"

"Nurse took them to bed at seven. It is now eleven."

"About seven-and-a-half o'clock, or it may have been eight, Mr. Olds, I heard some children singing outside the window, and I says to Mrs. Lirry, 'There are children singing;' but then it stopped, and when I went to the window I heard nothing. I remember the time, for

Henry just afterward started for Compton. It was just before the moon rose. Henry said he should have a good moon when he came back. I thought it was he when you came in. There he is now," and a wagon drove toward them, and the horse was reined in at such a strange concourse of people.

"Henry," said Mr. Olds, huskily, "have you met anybody? My children are lost."

"What! John and Peter and Jaky! Stop! what time was it?" and then he told how as he was driving off he heard some voices singing, and he stopped and listened, and saw three figures in a sort of whitey-brown covering, who chased each other down the Morris road, and he went on.

"That's them, no doubt," said Mr. Lirry, cheerfully. "They're taken care of at some farm-house, you may be sure; nothing but honest folks live down there. Come, Henry, jump out, and, Mr. Olds, you and Mrs. Olds take the wagon and drive down that way, so's to bring them home nicely."

"No," said Mr. Olds. "We don't know how long we may have to look. Henry's horse has been to Compton and back, and is tired. I shall harness my horse in the carryall and take everything that may be needed. Becky, go back to the house and get cordials and blankets. Give me the lantern — Rachel, you will come with me."

They turned back, and were soon by the house again, when Becky went in, but Mrs. Olds would stay by her husband. He carried the lantern, and they went out to the barn.

"Rachel," said he, as she clung to his arm, "it could not be that our children should suffer any harm on Christmas. I'm not superstitious, but it's Christmas, you know." Just then the clock struck twelve in the clear air, and at once, too, the bells were merrily rung, to usher in Christmas Day.

"O Jacob," said she, bitterly, "what right have we to expect God will take care of our children? Hark!" and she seized his arm convulsively. They stood dumb upon the threshold of the door.

"They found a babe" —

It was little Jacob who had suddenly waked at the sound of bells, and had sung the words that were last on his lips. It was their father's barn to which they had come back in their wanderings. He sang both verses clearly.

"Rachel," said Mr. Olds, "I dare not go in," and he sank down on the floor. But at that moment, the other children waking, began talking and crying together, and Mrs. Olds, opening the door, cried, as she looked into the darkness, —

"My children, my children!"

"Here we are, mamma," spoke up little Jacob. "O, I thought perhaps the babe had come. Do you really think he will come to-night? Nurse told us about him, but it was a secret. There was One who was found just so, when the angels sang to the shepherds, and He was good to people, and He died."

"And Johnny was Parson Dawes," broke in Peter, who was crying, and was very sleepy.

"Why didn't you hear us when we sang?" said John. "We sang real loud, and I pounded with my stick. This is the way we did," and the children, now wide awake, and standing on the barn-floor, sang once again their Christmas carol. And Becky, who had come out, said nothing, and could not even sing with them in her old cracked voice.

The next day was Sunday and Christmas. The three wise little boys did not know much about the King of the Jews whom they went to worship. But they went, nevertheless, and they carried, though they did not know it, some very precious offerings.

## TOM AND JOM.

THERE were two horses that drew a street car over rails in the city. They looked exactly alike, except that one had a white spot over his tail, and this was the only way that the stable-men and driver could tell him from the other, and yet they were quite different. The name of the one distinguished by the white mark was Tom; the name of the other was John. So the driver and the stable-men called him; but he was rather deaf, and, like deaf people, apt to seem a little dull. He thought his name was Jom, and that the driver, and stable-men, and Tom, who was always next to him, called him by that name.

They had travelled together, Tom and Jom, as long as either could remember, and were getting to be somewhat old; still they jogged on in the same track with a rattling car at their heels, day after day. They went down one street and up another, and into a third for a very long way; and after stopping a short while, started off again, and soon were in the first street again; and down that they went, and up the other, and so round and round, only at noon stopping for a lunch, and at night stopping for rest; the next day they started out and got into the middle of the track, and the car was hung on to them, and off they jogged again, rain or shine, hot or cold, down the street and up the next, and into the third.

As Tom and Jom moved along, they wagged their heads, and shook their tails a little; but they could not see each other very well, since they wore old-fashioned blinders. So they looked ahead. Yet they could talk to one another for all that. Tom liked talking best in the evening, when it was quiet about them, and he did not have to raise his voice so much; but Jom liked rather to talk in the day-time, when carts were rattling about them, because, like other deaf people, he could hear better then. So it was that one day when they had started out on their regular journey, they fell into conversation.

"Well," said Jom, "we seem to be going again — eh, Tom?"

"O don't talk yet," complained Tom. "Do wait till evening. It's so noisy. Besides, I feel so stupid always in the morning."

"Yes," said Jom, who was a little apt to repeat himself, — "yes, we seem to be going again. We've got a good long day before us, a good long day."

"Just hear him," groaned Tom. "I say, John!" he shouted.

"Well?" said Jom.

"Don't you wish it was night?"

"You needn't speak so loud. I hear well enough in the day-time. Why, do you think we shall get there then — eh, Tom? It looks like it. We've been going so long now, we must be 'most there. Let me see: yesterday and day before, and then day before that, and then the day those men were trying to get up those two long black things, that always seem to be going just ahead of us. O, no doubt we are almost there!" and he waggled his head sagely.

"I never did see such a —!" cried Tom. "You don't suppose it will be any different to-morrow, do you?"

"Why yes, if we get there."

"But we sha'n't get there."

"I don't know about that; we've been a-going now pretty long."

"But that's just it, John. Do we get ahead any?"

"Look here, Tom; look at my feet. Don't they step out a little farther along each time? It makes me almost dizzy to look at them. As sure as my name's Jom, we shall get there, depend upon it; yes, depend upon it — eh, Tom?" and Jom tried to look round his black spectacles at Tom.

"It's no use talking to that John," Tom muttered to himself. "If he thinks he is going anywhere where he won't have to begin and go all over again, his name is Jom and not John. I wish this old thing behind us would stop forever. I don't see why they fasten it on us. We don't do anything with it. And then it keeps stopping so, and it has such a horrible rattle."

Just then there was a sharp ring at the bell, and the brakes were put on.

"Hoh!" said Jom, who was tired of keeping his tongue still. "It's stopping to think, Tom — stopping to think. That's a queer chattering sound it makes. I wonder what it's going to do next? Ah! there it goes again," for the bell rang, the brakes were set free, and off they went.

"Tom," continued Jom, when they were once more well under way, "I've something to tell you."

"I wish it was dinner-time," cried Tom; "you always have something to tell me. I wish I was dead — I do. I'm a perfect slave. I remember when I was ridden for pleasure; yes, ridden about by little boys. They never hung one of these dreadful, jingling, rasping, heavy things behind me; and I could see out of the side of my eye, too. I don't care. I want some dinner."

"But, Tom," said Jom, mildly, "that was a long while ago; we're going to have something better now, something better — eh, Tom?"

"Something bitter!" said Tom, sharply.

"Yes, that's it, that's it," said Jom, reaching over playfully to caress Tom, "something better, something better." But the driver jerked the rein, and called out, —

"Heh there, John; mind now."

"Singular!" said Jom to himself; "whenever I want to rub my nose on Tom, there is the queerest hitch at the back of my head. But, Tom," he continued aloud, "really, now, I've something important to tell. Want to hear — eh, Tom? Do you remember that day the thing behind got tired, and couldn't move for a good while?"

"I remember how I thought we never should get home."

"Well, as we were standing, there was a vegetable cart near by, and I talked with the horse. He was a good, plain sort of horse. He didn't seem to think much, though, of the vegetables he had. I said how green they were. He said he couldn't see them himself, but he didn't like to smell them. He was used to grass. Just think, Tom, he had grass at home; and he wasn't such a very fine horse, either — not such a very fine horse. You used to have grass, I think you said?"

"Of course I did," said Tom.

"Well, he said that near where he lived there were — what do you guess? eh, what do you guess, Tom?"

"I don't guess anything."

"No, that wasn't it; they were — car horses, just like us! What do you think of that?"

"Well, we're not the only wretches."

"O, but they were eating grass," said Jom, and he raised his upper lip, and tried again to look round his black spectacles at Tom. "Now! Do you think we never shall get there?"

"No, we never shall; sure as your name's John."

"Well, sure as my name's Jom, as you say, I know we shall. I feel it every time that thing behind us begins to rattle so, and then stop to think. Sometimes, too, when I am not so deaf as usual, I hear a little tinkle sound behind. It seems to say, 'grass!'"

"Heigh ho!" said Tom. "Here we are at last. Now for dinner; and thank fortune I sha'n't have to listen to old Jom, as he calls himself, for an hour now."

The two horses were put into their stalls, and given their dinner. There was some talking going on about them; and presently, to Jom's surprise, he was led out of his stall. Where was he going? He went out of the stable, into the street, and then a man in a wagon took the halter-strap that was about his neck, and off they started, man and wagon, and behind, Jom, who felt unusually bright. He listened for the thing behind him. He could not hear it; and on they went without stopping, so that he was almost out of breath. They passed a vegetable wagon standing by the side of a shop.

"What! so you're going, too?" asked the vegetable horse, turning his head and recognizing Jom.

"Ye-ye-yes," nodded Jom, his head going up and down, as it always did when he was in delight.

"I'll see you to-night," called out the vegetable horse after him. But he did not see him. Jom was going into the country, but into another part. When the sun was going down, they came to a pretty house with a grassy slope before it. Children were playing about, rolling over the hay-cocks, and laughing in great sport.

"There he is! there he is!" they cried together, as the wagon came up, and they crowded down to the farmer.

"Is this really our new horse?" they asked. The father came up.

"Well, Coleman, he has a good character — has he?"

"O, bless you, sir, they say they never touched a whip to him. He's as gentle as a lamb. He's a bit stupid, sir, I'm thinking."

"No, I'm not stupid," said Jom, gravely. "I'm deaf."

But they did not heed him.

The children came closer, and patted him timidly. Jom raised his upper lip, and shook his head up and down, and said, "Come closer, children."

"What's his name, Mr. Coleman?" asked the oldest.

"It's Jom," said Jom.

"Well, I don't believe his mother ever gave him any," said the farmer.

"Let's call him June. It's the first day of June now." So they agreed to call him June.

"Jume? that's not exactly it," said he to himself, "but it will do. How I wish Tom was here.

"Curious!" said the father to the farmer; "how much this old horse looks like one I once had. The only difference that I can see is that that one had a white spot over his tail."

"That was Tom," broke in Jom, eagerly, who heard the last few words.

"I used to ride him when I was a boy; but he had a bad temper, was a fretful, impatient horse, and we sold him."

"O, then it wasn't Tom," said Jom to himself.

"Now, please, put me on his back!" cried the oldest; "and me," pleaded the next; "and me," "and me:" so old Jom was soon walking round delighted, with the children on his back; and he smelt the sweet grass, and even ventured to put his nose down and nibble a little.

Happy Jom! Poor Tom!

## THE VISION OF JOHN THE WATCHMAN.

When the stars are shining on a December night, and that night is the last of the year that runs from Christmas to Christmas, then is the time for new thoughts to be born; everything is transparent, everything that sounds has a clear ring to it. One looks over the country, and the trees seem watching for what the gray dawn may reveal to the world; and if one must walk down city streets, there, too, the very houses stand higher, as if to hear what may be sounding above; and the church spires listen to catch the first note. As twelve o'clock comes on, the stillness deepens; every click upon the pavement sounds like the beating of a stony heart. What will come? what will be seen and heard when the new year begins on Christmas Day?

The top of Trinity spire would seem to be the best place for a watchman at such a time. From that dizzy height, he could peer off over the water, or over the land, following the lines of twinkling lights below, or up into the sky, ready for the first breath of sound or glimpse of heavenly sight; and then from that perch he could make his voice dart down and into the belfry, and down by other voices, till glad hands should pull at the chiming bells to summon all who might be listening and waiting and watching, on Christmas Eve.

But on one memorable Christmas Eve, memorable for our John the Watchman, there was no one thus lifted up above the common streets, or who can say what good news might have been sounded over the city? and yet — would he have seen what John saw? Now, John was a watchman — that was his business. Every night when the gas was lighted, John put on his great watch-coat, pulled his cap well on, kissed the children and Mary his wife, and with a stout brown paper parcel in his pocket, which Mary had stowed there, set off for Church Street, to keep watch over a great warehouse.

How much money there was in that warehouse! not in gold, and silver, and copper, but in stone, which rose, story above story, up toward the sky; and inside, in cloth, and wonderful fabrics of every kind. All day long, scores of clerks went about in it, selling goods; or sat and stood, silently pinned to desks, like dead butterflies all in a row, as they added up columns of figures, till their heads ached, and found out every day how much money the warehouse was worth; and every day, gray-haired, sharp-eyed old gentlemen sat where they could see the row of butterflies, and looked over their shoulders, and found out how much they owned, — for they owned the warehouse; and then when the gas out-of-doors was lighted, they took the pins out, and the butterfly clerks went home, and the old gentlemen went home, and the porter locked all the doors, and he went home; and then John came, and he stayed, — till the porter came back next morning.

The first thing John the Watchman always did, was to go round to all the doors, and try them, take hold of the handles, and pull and rattle them; and Peter the Inside Watchman — for there was one inside and one out — Peter would hear it, and say to himself, — "Good! there's John: all right!" Then when John had tried all the doors, he looked at the windows, to see if they were fastened; and he poked his stick into all the gratings, but that was only because it seemed a safe thing to do, for what could happen about a grating that a stick could poke into? Then he settled into his great-coat, felt of the bundle in his pocket, and now he was all right for the night, and he began to walk up and down, down and up, round the square, back and forth, always changing his course, so as to turn up unexpectedly everywhere, and be always on the spot, should any one be so bold as to try a door with a false key, or think to take out a light of glass. A quick robber he would be, who came round the corner and did not find John the Watchman at that post.

Now, on this night, John settled himself as usual into his shaggy coat, and began his steady beat over the flagging. There was no snow on the ground. It was a clear, cold night; the bright stars were shining in the heavens, which spanned the earth with a pure blue arch; blue indeed, this night, as any one could see who looked up. The air was still, and every sound that stirred came sharp upon the ear. Broadway, not far off, seemed to be a procession of sounds of every sort and kind, while just about John's walk, it was long before the street was clear, — so many people went briskly by, and carts and omnibuses clattered past. It was a lively evening, and John watched the sights about him, and wondered and wondered, — what this one had in his basket — how many children that old gentleman had — whether he had anything in his pockets for them. You see John's mind rather ran upon children. He had two, twins, a girl and a boy, John and Mary, just his own and wife's names, so they were called Little John and Mary Little. It is hard to get away from these twins, now that we have begun to talk about them; but we must: we have nothing to do with them to-night, except as we look into our John's — John the Big's — mind, for in that mind are stowed the twins. They are safe in bed now at home, and safe in John's mind at the same time. But it is extraordinary how fast they grow! Now, children grow when they sleep, every one knows that; and while the twins, just a year old, are laid in their little bed, Mary is watching them, and John the Watchman is watching them in his mind, off by the warehouse. As they look steadily at them, how fast they grow! It is only eight o'clock now, and John is seeing in his mind's eye — for that is what looks on in the mind — John is seeing a great John and Mary: a stout young man, who has grown up in three hours, like Jack of the Bean-stalk; a wonderful young man, who has been at college, and knows so much — dear me! John the Watchman begins to wonder whether son John will not think his father dreadfully ignorant, and a foolish old man. And he sees Mary, now Mary the Tall, a fair young woman, as beautiful as her mother, moving about so gracefully, that the old house looks very homely for so charming a maid to live in; and John sighs to himself, and then starts with a laugh, and in a twinkling, John the Wise and Mary the Tall are back in their cradle again, with their thumbs in their mouths. They have been growing just in the same way, as Mary looks at them.

The passers in the street gradually were fewer and fewer: the changing noises in Broadway died down; the lights, except in the street lamps disappeared one by one, and still John kept his pacing by the great warehouse. He looked up now and then at the windows of the hospital which stood near by. He often looked there, and tried to fancy what the people behind were doing. He would see forms pass and repass, get up and sit down, and he knew that behind those stone and brick walls there were many poor sufferers, who tossed restlessly through the night, and wished that morning would come, — morning, that brought nothing but a change of pain. He could see a light in one of the windows now. There were people moving about in the room, slowly, and it seemed to him very gently. He saw a woman pour out a draught by the light, and carry it — to the sufferer on the bed, he did not doubt; and John fell to thinking how many people there must be, rich and poor, who were sick that night, and he was well and walking about. John was a simple sort of a man. When he thought of this, he looked up for a moment, and thanked God that he was well. Then he began to think about Little John and Mary Little. What if they should be taken sick, and this very night! and he went on and prayed to God to take care of John and Mary.

Click! click! click! a sharp tap three times on the sidewalk. The same sound again. John the Watchman knew what it meant. He must stay at his post, but all about came hurrying the city watchmen, with their clubs in their hands. He heard a noise, cries, terrible words, sharp blows. It was confusion; but he knew that there, down the street, a fight was going on. Presently a squad of men came up the street, dragging a fierce, ragged man, who gesticulated and shouted; behind, came shortly another body of men, bearing on their shoulders a wounded man, while an angry, cowardly gang of men, women, and boys hung about, or turned and fled, when it seemed as if they would be pursued. Tramp, tramp, they went past John the Watchman.

"What is it?" he asked in a low tone.

"Stabbing!" said one of the men, and on they went, the wild man screaming, the wounded man groaning, as he was borne painfully along.

John trembled as they left him. He could not help it; he was not a coward — let any one try the warehouse and see! but John had just been thinking about Little John and Mary Little. He thought of them again, and shuddered. He seemed to see them in that crowd. He looked up at the warehouse. It was bolted and secured at every point. There was money, he knew, behind those stone and iron walls. He was set there to watch, because wicked men there were, who would risk life to rob the warehouse. He heard the screaming man, whom the officers could not quiet, as they dragged him along, and of a sudden it seemed to him that the city was full of wicked men and women. And this was Christmas Eve, and how long it was since He had come to save the world. More than eighteen hundred years, and was this all? How could he, with his fatherly heart, keep Little John and Mary Little from ending like this? John was a simple man; he prayed to God to keep the children from sin. Let them be sick and suffer, if need be, he said, but keep them from sin.

John looked earnestly up and around. He saw the bolted warehouse. There was all that money; and yet people, if they could go in and take it all, would not be made righteous by that. There was the hospital. Good people built it and watched in it; but they could not keep their own children from sickness. And John whispered to himself, — No! they could not keep their own children from sin. There stood the dim outline of a church. People could go in and out: did that keep them right?

Poor John began to be dizzy, as he thought of these things. "Why, what can keep us right?" he cried aloud. "God is so far off. He sees us and hears us, but we can't see Him. How can I be sure that Little John and Mary Little will be right, and keep right?" and he saw the twinkling stars, and the clear blue sky, and the thought rushed over him, — Only the pure in heart shall see God.

"Lord God!" he cried. "How long? how long?"

Did the blue sky open? was there a movement among the stars? John the Watchman, resting for a moment from his tramp, leaning against the warehouse door, heard no sound, and the street and hospital were there still; and yet, in the street, above it, in heaven or on earth, who could tell? he saw the form of One like the Son of Man. He did not fear to look upon Him, for every line in that face and form drew his eyes. He saw Him pass, and touch a poor man bending over a heap of garbage, who looked up into His face, and straightway caught, in faint resemblance, the same look, and John for one moment glanced at the rag-picker with the changed face. But back he turned to the One, who passed now over the threshold of a church. He saw Him enter. He saw the bowed heads of the multitude; and when they looked up, though He was gone, their faces gave back a little of the kindling glory. Once more he saw Him lift the latch of a humble house, and enter there. O joy! it was John's own house. There sat Mary, bending over the sleeping babes. He saw Him look upon the mother, and then upon the children. Did He smile? from the little faces came a smile. There was no solitude when He was gone; He took away no blessing with Him. Down through dark streets John saw

Him pass, lighting the way as He moved. Men, and women, and children gathered around Him. Alas! for those who shut their eyes, and turned again to slumber. Did they know that he was there? Yet he left a light in the place, — He left faces of holiness. Ever and ever John saw Him pass and repass; brighter and brighter shone the light about Him. The city's hum sounded, yet He did not go; there was a vast moving, hither and thither, of busy men and women; the streets of the city were full of boys and girls, playing in the streets thereof; and yet, go where they would, their eyes were still turned upon Him. He went where each went; they were walking beside Him.

Was this heaven? was this earth? John the Watchman looked through it all, and, as his eyes peered more steadily, solid shapes held them. A light moved in a casement, forms flitted back and forth. He was aware of familiar objects. The hospital was before him. He stood firmly upon the sidewalk, and looked anxiously at the lighted window. There he had seen the ministering woman, and felt the sick man to be. Now he could see plainly that there were several in the room. He saw them kneel by the bedside.

"It is his last moment," said John to himself. They knelt, and then all rose but one, — the woman, — and she kept her place.

"Lord Jesus, receive his spirit," murmured John.

Hark! on the kneeling woman, and on John the Watchman murmuring his prayer, struck the sound of chiming bells.

Still here! still here! they joyfully rang. Lo, He cometh! In clouds, in clouds!

Louder and louder pealed the bells, while full in John the Watchman's heart sounded the glad tidings — He is the life of the world. Men shall look upon Him and live. The Jesus Christ of Galilee and Jewry, — He that was lifted up — He would draw all men unto Him.

Christmas morning had risen.

## THE STORY THAT NEVER WAS TOLD.

In the middle of the garden was a lake, and in the middle of the lake was an island, and in the middle of the island was a bower, and there sat a Little Girl. No hands had made the bower, but some rhododendrons grew in a circle and dropped their flaming flowers upon a mound of earth, which was the Little Girl's seat. There was room within the bower for a great many visitors, and through the opening in front one could see, or at least the Little Girl could see, over the water, and out toward the mountains that stood in the wide world.

She could see down the slope, too, that led from the bower to the lake, and thus she saw the procession that wound up the path to where she sat. She watched it come and her heart beat lightly, for she knew that now she was to hear stories; yes, each one in the procession was to tell a story — a story about the wide world where they lived. And off on the lake she could see a tiny boat — only a speck in the distance — that had spread its white sails and was coming toward her. Were there more story-tellers in the boat? that she could not tell; but nearer came the troop winding along the path.

Tra-la-la! tra-la-la-la! the Columbine horns were sounding; Thrum-thrum! droned the Burdock-leaves; Pweep-weep! whistled the cold Indian-pipe, and the Pea-pods burst in with their snapping Pop! pop!

They were coming, they were close by! and the Little Girl clapped her hands as the music stopped, and a kid and a kitten skipped up to the bower, and tumbled a little courtesy to her.

"Your name is Kid, and yours is Kitten," said the Little Girl. "Tell me, Kitten, what they do in the wide world where you live."

"O," said Kitten, "we play. Shall I tell you a story? Yesterday we played we were playing. T'other Kitty — that's not me, but the Kitty that didn't come to-day — T'other Kitty and I had a ball, and we played that we were playing with this ball. It was all in fun, you know: we only played we were playing. I tossed it to T'other Kitty, and she tossed it to me; then I tossed it to her, and she tossed it to me; and then I tossed it to her, and she tossed it to me; and then I played I tossed it to her, and she played she tossed it to me; and then I played that I was a Kitty tossing a ball to T'other Kitty, and she played she was a Kitty tossing a ball to me; and then I played that I was a Kitty playing that I was tossing a ball that played it was a ball" —

"O, O!" said the Little Girl; "and what came next?"

"And then T'other Kitty went away, and I played that I was playing" —

Just then the Little Boy who had come up in the procession put his head into the bower.

"Mayn't I tell my story?" said he.

"No," said the Little Girl. "You must wait. I am going to hear the Kid now. Kid, Kid, what can you tell me?"

"Shall I tell you where I went yesterday? I saw a rock, and I went skip, skip, to reach it. It was a steep rock, it had little jogs in it, and I skipped from one jog to another, till I was a-top of it."

"And what did you do then?"

"I saw the kid" — began the Little Boy, eagerly.

"Hush! What did you do then, Kid?"

"O, I skipped down from one jog to another, and then I went skip, skip, home again."

"I have so much to tell" —

"Little Boy, you must wait. Now" —

"Chip, chip!" twittered the swallows that came flying into the bower, and darting in and out. "Chip, chip! we know what the world is. We have flown about it. You go up into the blue, then you skim along, and there it is!"

"But what is the world like? Can you tell me no story?" asked the Little Girl.

"Yes, yes, we know. We have flown about it. You go up into the blue, then you skim along, and there it is."

"I have a secret," said the Little Boy.

"By and by, Little Boy."

"But it is about the swallows. I have been with them."

"Be quiet. I feel quite sure that I shall now hear something worth hearing. Hush, music. Ant! Bee!"

"We have no time to idle, but we tell you a story," began the Ant and Bee together. "It may do you good. Listen! There were once two ants and two bees. One ant and one bee played all the time. The other ant and the other bee worked all the time. Do you see those corpses? that is an ant and that is a bee. Do you see that tree? There is a store of honey in it, and there is an ant-hill at the bottom. That is OUR honey, and OUR hill. We are the other ant and the other bee. Good by."

"But stop!" said the Little Girl. "You have told me nothing of the world where you live."

"That is OUR honey and OUR hill," said the Ant and the Bee as they went off.

"I have been there. I can tell you," began the Little Boy.

"That is OUR honey and OUR hill," said the Ant and the Bee in the distance.

"Hark!" said the Little Girl, putting her hand behind her ear.

"That is OUR honey and OUR hill."

"I can just hear them," said she. "Dear me, I don't think I quite understand."

"I will explain" —

"Stand aside, Little Boy, we will explain." There were three this time, that came up together, but they were of different sizes. The Cow was the largest, and the Mouse was the smallest, and the Rabbit came in between. Nevertheless, it was not easy to say which was the wisest. They stood in a row, and the Cow began: —

"As soon as I have finished swallowing I

will tell all about it. Everything that is worth knowing comes with me. I do not take it all in at once, but I try it. I test it, and if it is worth keeping I swallow it. I heard what the Ant and the Bee said, and I took it in; but I have not swallowed it yet. You may be sure that it is worth something if I swallow it."

"But at least you can tell me a story, Rabbit," said the Little Girl, as the Cow now went on swallowing.

"Certainly," said the Rabbit, "certainly. It shall be a fable. No story is of value except it be a fable. A story — something made up out of one's head about nothing — bah! it is only fit for children."

"And yet," — began the Little Boy.

"Patience, Little Boy. I think I will hear you soon."

"A fable," went on the Rabbit, — "a fable has a meaning. It is about the world. It is not a story, for it has a moral at the end, and who ever saw a story with a moral at the end?" and he looked round with his pink eyes at the company. The Mouse, who had been sitting upright in order better to be seen, went forward and whisked his tail.

"A fable," he piped, "is like a mouse. It has a tail."

"How dare you?" said the Rabbit.

"And a story is like a rabbit. If it has a tail it is driven inside. The tail is everything. A fable has a tail. A story has no tail."

The Rabbit was very angry.

"A tail!" he exclaimed. "A tail! what is a tail? Have I a tail, and am I nothing? Is a tail everything? a tail! indeed! a tail!"

"But I have not heard your fable," said the Little Girl timidly. "I wanted a story, but if a fable is so much better" —

"I know a fable" — eagerly began the Little Boy.

"I know about you, sir," said the Mouse quietly. I advise you to wait. If you have not succeeded in having your say yet, you never will get it. Your time is gone by. You belong to the Little Boys. Do you know how old I am?" he added sharply, looking with his keen eyes into the Little Girl's face.

"I think you are old enough to teach me a good deal."

"Humph! Do you see this stone I am sitting on? Under that stone there are some beetles. Under the beetles there is the earth. Under the earth — what?" and he looked round on the company. No one answered.

"What?" he repeated. "What is under the earth?"

"I've swallowed it!" said the Cow, who had been chewing all this time with her eyes half shut.

"Dear, dear," said the Little Girl. "What was it?"

"A tail!" mumbled the Rabbit. "A tail everything!"

"What is under the earth?" demanded the Mouse; and the Cow only stood still and said nothing.

"Let me see," said the Little Girl, putting her hand over her eyes; "it was about the Ant and the Bee."

"Yes," said the Cow, "that was it. I swallowed it."

"And you said it would be worth nothing unless you swallowed it?"

"Yes," said the Cow; "that is it."

"Then tell me about it," said the Little Girl, getting a little impatient.

"It's gone," said the Cow. "I've swallowed it."

"You can get nothing out of her, do you not see?" said the Little Boy. "Surely now you will listen to me!"

"Not so fast, Little Boy," spoke up a harsh voice, which was followed by a succession of little subdued cluckings, and a great Rooster rose up before them, followed at a respectful distance by a hen and eleven chickens.

"I am here, Little Girl."

"Then speak out," said she, "and tell me what the world is. I want no more stories;" and the Little Girl seemed to speak almost in the tones of the Rooster himself.

"The world! The world is a dunghill. I scratch it!" and a heap of dust flew over the hen and chickens behind him. "There is a living in it. But what of that? It is good for nothing except to rule over. You have the island. I have the world. When I like, I shall kick it behind me. It is nothing. I scratch it." And another little cloud of dust flew over the humble hen and chickens, while the Rooster set up a defiant crow.

There was silence.

"Alas!" said the Little Girl weeping; "what has become of the boat? I saw it until now coming toward me, and I felt sure that it would contain something better than these. Little Boy, can you see the boat?"

"Come with me," said he, "and you also shall see it," and he took her by the hand and led her down from the mound and out of the bower. As she came forth the music which had been so long silent, struck up faintly.

"Tra-la-la! thrum! pweep! pop!"

But the Little Boy opened his mouth and sang. The words were not many; they were simple, too, but the music of his voice made them of worth. And as he sang, the Little Girl listened and they went further away from all the story-tellers, down toward the shore.

Then he told her stories.

He told her of a happy day when the sun shone bright, and he was dancing over the fields, and suddenly a new light that was not from the sun, fell upon a rose which he was plucking, and he would not pluck the rose. Then he told her how he was once floating down the river in a boat, listening to sweet music, when one of the notes seemed to wander off from the rest, and to rise and rise until it touched the sky, when the sky opened, and as the little note was lost to hearing a great company of heavenly sounds received it. And then he told her how he had once gone down into the bed of a stream and found gold, gold so precious that when it was crumbled it turned into land and houses, and bread and drink, and the poor had been fed and clothed, and the sick and suffering had cordials and comforts. But there was another story still which he told, of what he saw as he lay at night and watched the stars. He saw them come forth one by one, and he began to count them, and as he counted them they disappeared one by one, and when the last was gone there shone forth another star above him, which was so near that it seemed to him he could touch it, and yet so far away that its light seemed forever travelling toward him.

"Will you hear another story?" asked the Little Boy. "It is my last. In the middle of the garden was an island, and in the middle of the island was a bower, and there sat a Little Girl. The Kid and the Kitten sported before her to make her think that the world was all a frolic; the Swallows flew about her, for the world was all an idle flight to them; the Ant and the Bee left their hoarding to show her that the world was a hollow tree full of riches; the Cow and the Rabbit and the Mouse came together to wag their wisdom, and show that the world was nothing but something to think about; the Rooster came to make her see that the world was only good for anything as it made her proud, and so as she looked and looked the Little Girl became blind. Then she wept but she could not see, and then the Little Boy kissed her eyes" —

"Ah!" said the Little Girl, "I see now."

"What do you see?" he asked.

"I see you, Love."

"And nothing else?" said Love, sorrowfully.

The Little Girl did not turn her eyes, but she looked up and said joyfully, —

"I see the boat that once I saw."

"Come!" and he took her by the hand as they went toward the boat.

"Can I leave the island?" said she, looking back wistfully.

"You have not heard all of the stories yet," said he smiling.

"Then I shall hear more from you!"

They entered the boat and sailed away over the water. More stories were told on the island, but there was one story that never was told. It was the story of what befell the Little Girl who sailed away. Eye hath not seen, nor ear heard, neither hath entered the heart of man to conceive what happened afterwards to the Little Girl who sailed away.

ROMANCE.

# ROSE AND ROSELLA.

## I.

In the King's garden were all manner of strange and beautiful plants. One might wander over it, and fancy he had visited all quarters of the globe, for there was nothing so rare but the Gardener would obtain it, and give it, if need be, a house all to itself in the great garden; and not content with having what he found, he was perpetually seeking to produce some new kind of flower, which one would search the world through in vain to find elsewhere. Everything was wonderfully contrived, everything was under the most perfect care; and in the palace, when the guests were tired of dancing and feasting, they would say, "Come, let us go into the garden, and see what new thing the Gardener has."

The Gardener himself was there, all day long, walking about the paths, dressed in a flowing, flowered gown, with a pruning-knife in his hand, looking so sharply at each plant, as he went by, that one could easily see it would fare hard with them if they did not mind him. The guests would follow after and look at the plants he stopped before, and smell, and shut one eye, and look grave, but they never dared pluck a single bud. The King said openly that he cared nothing for flowers after they were gathered, and so he never plucked any, though of course he could, for it was his garden.

Now there was in the garden one plant which was reckoned above all the rest in value. It had a house over its head, and was watched by the Gardener more closely than any other. Thither his feet always turned when he took his tour; and the guests, those who were wise, would look at each other and say, — "Well, shall we go and look at the Rosella?" The King even, would inquire in the morning how the Rosella fared — the mock Rosella, he would sometimes explain good-naturedly, looking at the Princess, — but that was when the Gardener was not there, and the King was familiar.

The Rosella was a rose, a rose so wonderful that there was not another in the kingdom, and so not another in the whole world, that could for a moment be compared with it. The

Gardener had therefore given it the name of the Princess Rosella, the only one in the royal family beside the King and Queen. The Princess Rosella was as peerless among women as the flower Rosella was among roses, and a decree had gone forth that no one in the kingdom should bear that name, and that it should not be bestowed upon any flower or bird, so that it passed into proverb—Worthy to bear the name of Rosella.

The King and Queen had selected from the neighboring princes, one of high renown and great possessions, whom they were willing to accept as the Princess's suitor, and the day was at hand when the ceremony of betrothal was to take place. Rosella, indeed, had never beheld the Prince, but she had heard for months of the Prince's famous horses, of his chariot, of his buglers, and of the magnificent palace to which he would one day conduct her, where she would rule the court. The King had a fancy that the betrothal should take place on the day when the consummate flower of the Rose should unfold its petals; it was to be worn by the Princess, and the world should then behold such splendor of beauty as never before was known, when the Princess Rosella, loveliest of the lovely, should appear before the court, adorned with the Rosella Rose, most glorious of glorious flowers.

Every one watched eagerly for the promise which the Rose should give of the final flowering forth, and every day tidings were brought of what new growth and expansion were observed, until at length it was announced by heralds that on the morrow the betrothal would take place in the presence of the great court, and all who were to take part were bidden prepare for the festival.

II.

On the morning before the betrothal, the Rose, silently breathing and unfolding, stood in its sheltered home, guarded from sea-winds, and bathed in a gentle atmosphere tempered to its need. What more could flower desire? what higher place could be given it on earth? opening its heart to the tender air about it, and borne at last upon the bosom of the most splendid of the daughters of earth. Yet thoughts, fancies, feelings, memories were wrapped in the opening leaves, quite other than seemed to befit this favored flower.

Its silent surroundings were broken now by footfalls drawing near, and entering the house came the Gardener, and with him a young man who had never before been in the presence of the Rose. They stood before it, and the Gardener said, —

"Behold, Master Philip, the Rosella."

The young man bowed.

"Hear her history. I found her a paltry rose by the sea-shore, growing carelessly with so many others, not to be distinguished by ordinary eyes. However, I had not formed the King's garden for nothing. I saw in the thin, impoverished flower a germ of something fairer, and I resolved that human art should not fail of transforming the wild, country rose into a flower meet for kings' palaces. Whatever art and experience could give me I laid before this plant. When you see this bud fairly open, then, Master Philip, if you have eyes, you will read in its leaves sixteen years of sun and air and earth made obedient. Reproduce the rose you cannot, but I have called you in that you may preserve for the world something of the glory of the Rosella Rose when it has passed away. Bring also, your art to the feet of this Rose, and lay on your wood if you can, some faint portraiture of its transcendent beauty. Your time is short; to-morrow at mid-day, the Rose-bud now unfolding must be plucked by my hand, and given to the

Princess as she goes to receive the Prince her betrothed."

The young Painter, for such he was, answered lightly, —

"Have no fear, Master Gardener, the Rose shall grow again on my panel," and he sat down before it, humming to himself. Again were steps heard, and now came the King and Queen, who were taking their morning walk, and must needs regard the Rose. The Gardener made his obeisance, and proceeded to explain the presence of the young man who was working steadily on.

"It is a humble friend of mine," he said, in a low tone, "who has shown some skill in painting, and whom I have employed to make a picture of the Rosella Rose, that I may have something to show when the original is gone. He is a worthy young man whom I can trust here."

The King nodded and advanced to where the Painter sat.

"Work on, young man," said he. "Don't mind me. A king is a king, and a rose is a rose. Now I dare say you will make this handsome. Pluck a rose, leave a rose, rose it is still."

"You know, perhaps," put in the Queen,

"that the Rose is to be worn by the Princess at her betrothal? That takes place to-morrow, I suppose. Dear me! how the world goes round; I shall be glad when it is over," and the Queen, who was heated, fanned herself with a peacock feather fan.

"Expect nothing, and nothing will trouble you," said the King, sagely. "If now, we were to begin to wonder what would happen if the Princess should decide to have her own way, when the question was asked, what folly it would be. Easy come, easy go. Knock an apple down with a stick and eat it; climb the tree and the worm has ate it. When the stone begins to roll, get behind it."

"Well, I never can answer you," said the Queen; "but it don't make things go right to let them take care of themselves. Come, let us look after Rosella."

The couple went away, and the Gardener looked at the Painter carefully.

"There are some things," said he, "that even kings do not know. Gardening is one, and — pictures are another."

"Well," said Philip, with a laugh, "one may not be a king, and yet be ignorant. Does the Princess also pay visits to the Rose?"

"Hark! there she is coming now. I think

I will go for a watering-pot," and to the Painter's surprise, the Gardener went hastily out of the little house just as the Princess entered it. As she entered, Philip rose and bowed, and then stood until the Princess said: —

"Go on, master; we all obey the Rose here."

Philip took his place again before the panel, and as he worked, the Princess looked over his shoulder.

"When you paint that flower," said she, "do you think all the time what a fine thing it will be to have painted the Rosella Rose? Is it that makes you work so diligently?"

"O, I never find this irksome; though, to tell the truth, I should not probably have chosen this flower; but the Gardener set me down before it."

"And the Gardener will put the picture in his gallery, I suppose," said the Princess, mockingly.

"Is it strange that he should wish to keep some likeness of the flower which he has reared so carefully?

"O, that is well enough, I suppose. But tell me, do you see any beauty in that Rose? I do not. I think it is detestable."

"No flower," said the Painter, looking at

Rosella's beautiful face, now flushed with some secret temper, "no flower can be wholly ruined by man, when the rain and sun and kindly earth make up the great sum of its nourishment. Look at those leaves; the color is deepened, but human art had not done it, without nature had been willing to lend her aid."

"I think it is detestable," repeated the Princess, petulantly. "It grows uglier to me every time I see it. It looks as if the Gardener fed it with wine every hour. And yet," she added, sighing, "all the roses in the garden look in the same way. Tell me, have you ever seen anything different? Every one here goes about the garden with his hands up at every frightful green and yellow thing."

The Painter drew forth from a case a little painting which he laid in the Princess's hands. She looked long and wistfully at it. It was a picture of wild roses. Green flags rose to the eye, about which gathered a few solitary roses, open to sunlight, wind, and rain, their shell-like transparency deepening into a more glowing hue, as if along their tender veins ran at times the warmest life. They laid their faces against the broad flags, or peeped merrily at each other from behind them. Nothing of the country about or beyond could be seen; but the background of the picture had in it faint touches of color, now deeper green, now purple, now hazy distance, that made one, looking at it, begin to fancy, according to pleasure, the sweetest and most mysterious landscape.

She laid the picture down and went quietly out of the little house. Philip returned to his task. He was busy with thought, as his hands moved at work, and did not notice that the Princess returned, and was watching him. His lips began to move, and soon, half to himself, half aloud, came the words of a song: —

"Marina, Marina, my rose by the sea,
Come back, come back, come back to me."

The Princess touched him on the shoulder, then drew her hand hastily away.

"If you can paint such flowers, why do you paint this rose?"

"This also is a rose."

"This a rose! how unlike the Rosella!"

"Both like and unlike, lady. Once, years ago, as the Gardener tells me, this Rose which he cherishes so jealously, lived simply and freely in some pasture, or beside some brook. He saw in it the germ of a rich and elegant flower, and he brought it hither, resolved that it should some day excel in beauty and fame all the roses of the land. Behold the Rosella! You see only the Gardener's toil and art; but look more closely at this open bud beside my picture, and see if you cannot discover some recollection in it of its earlier days."

The Princess obeyed. As she looked steadfastly the Rosella seemed, in her imagination, to drop, one by one, its costly robes, to give back all that had been expended on it, to recover its lost simplicity and native freshness; looking no longer at the picture, but only at the flower she had despised, the Princess began to see faint outlines of a country where it seemed to dwell. Perhaps a humid veil before her eyes was the mist which seemed to rise over a stretch of sea; perhaps it was the remembrance of Philip's little picture which spread before her sight green meadow lands, and a rippling brook overhung with wild roses.

"Where did you paint this?" she at last asked.

Philip began, "Lady"—when steps were heard, and the King and Queen again entered the little Rose house.

"Well, Rosella," began the Queen, "we have searched for you this hour, and now we have at last reached you."

"Yes," said the King, "we have found her. Now there are no more troubles eh? Keep what you find, and forget what you lose."

"A pretty way, indeed," said the Queen, in a heat. "What comfort could one take then? Rosella, we must go. There is so much yet to be done, and that great assembly to-night. I wish in my heart it were over."

"Or never begun," suggested the King.

"No, indeed; of course it must be begun; but there is an end to everything."

"I am not so sure of that," said the King, walking off behind them.

Philip remained by the Rose till the sun went down. He was loath to leave it, and as he went away from it, a strange feeling began to possess him. He scarcely knew why, but it seemed to him he would rather remain by the Rose than meet again the mistress of the Rose. But once more in the free air, he stepped forth into heightened life. "Nay," said he, to himself, "I will have all, nor stop like a fool content to dream over the likeness of the thing itself."

Could he now have revisited the Rose, with the finer sense which some have, he might have observed its perturbation and listened to its sighing.

Alone in its treasure-house, the Rosella Rose, cherished with constant care, and separated from all meaner things, kept folding and unfolding its leaves, as thoughts rose and fell within its bosom. It needed not the words of the Gardener and their repetition by the Painter, for it to know that its secret life was something more than the Gardener had given it. But when Philip's picture was placed beside it, there stirred within its depths the old nature never yet driven forth by the Gardener's art. Again the sea-breeze sent strong, sinewy life through its fibres, the meadows stretched out under the blue sky, the little brook that coursed through them rippled under her living roots, and the tiny cock-boats which the children launched danced gayly down the stream; the children's laughter glanced through the bushes, their voices sought one another, and now pushing aside the twigs and osiers with their hands, their pretty faces peeped into the water, and looked up into the gentle roses that looked down on them from the bush.

III.

In the palace at evening the guests were all gathered, the lights shone brilliantly in hall and gallery and vaulted room. The music sounded far or near, as it obeyed the will of the band-master, who seemed to follow with his notes the passing footsteps of the throng who swarmed in and out. The King and Queen were there on the dais, and the Princess by them. The betrothing Prince was not there. He was with his retinue outside in camp, for he had not yet seen the Princess, and was not to see her until the morrow. But gentlemen from his court were there, who spread marvelous tales of all the splendid preparations that had been made for the Princess when she should finally enter her new realm; and it was whispered that the Prince would be a most obsequious consort, who would gallantly bow before the Princess at every step of her grand career. She was glorious indeed to look upon; rich in all the splendor which could be arrayed on her queenly form, and richer still in the deep color which ebbed and flowed in her restless face. Yet now and then a strange light stole into her eye, and it was as if she looked through the shadowy forms thronging around her, beyond the thin walls of the palace; but the soul thus sent out on its journeying came back again; the light died down, and some royal word fled from her lips which shot a courtier and made his face tingle with the wound.

"She is magnificent to-night," they whispered to one another.

"May the Prince prize her magnificence," thought the wounded courtier.

"Yes, splendid enough," was the response of one; "thank Heaven, we shall soon hear the end of Rosella."

"Plucked and thrown away at last," said another, jestingly. "The Rose and Rosella — will they have the same fortune?"

In the quiet of the night, Philip walked into the dark recesses of the garden, and hearing a brook, moved toward it, resting at length upon a rude bench beneath a willow, past which flowed the little stream, falling noiselessly over a sandy bed. As he watched and listened, his memory seemed to slip along with the movement of the waters, forth from the garden and the day into the world, out among other lands where he had wandered, to the place of his childhood, and from that faint remembrance, his mind travelled down again over his varied years to the King's garden and to the Princess Rosella.

A hand was laid on his shoulder and quickly withdrawn. He rose to his feet.

"Sit down, Master Philip," said the Princess, "and I will sit beside thee; I could not rest and I came here. This is my seat; I sit here often and look at the brook. It is a strange brook; I know not why it should flow over a sandy bed; it should have pebbles to flow over, and then it would sing. Did you ever hear a brook that flowed over pebbles?"

"Lady Rosella," said the Painter, looking still into the brook, "such simple things as I have seen and known have little charm for those that dwell in this palace or walk in the King's grounds. Yet something there is which belongs to all. This brook itself, so I must think," and he lifted his eyes as if he would search for its outlet — "this brook surely is the same which flows by my home, and loses itself in the meadows by the great sea. Beside it I have walked; I have listened to its voice; I have launched my childish craft in it and parted the bushes to see how the cockle boats fared, and found roses, such as I have painted in my picture, looking down into the water. But I did not know till now that the brook issued from the little spring above us here and flowed through the King's garden and out into the world."

"Tell me more of your home and of the sea-shore."

"The sea breaks upon the coast in long waves, and summer and winter one hears its unceasing fall; now violent and stormy, beating at the beach as if it would find entrance to some hidden world, now gently, as if laying down its weariness upon a friendly bosom. A promontory juts out like a great boar's head into the ocean, and there I have stood at the going down of the sun and looked westward over the marshes, where the tall reeds rise out of the muddy waters, and the wide waste seems aglow with some wondrous life which flames forth only as the day passes into the night."

"And who live by this strange place?"

"A few simple fishermen and sea-farers; my own parents were such; now they are gone, and there remains one only whom I care much to visit. He is my dearest earthly friend. He moved my soul with poetic words when the sea and the sky and the reedy marshes moved me with their language. He dwells alone, and in that little gathering of plain people, he is the voice that utters their best thoughts, and to him they come with their troubles and their joys; he says not much to them, but by and by they learn from him a song which is now to them their own heart, beating in words."

"Sing me one of his songs."

"I think of one that came to him in this wise. There was a fisherman who had a child, and the child died; and he thought to himself, —the living sea is better than the dark ground; so men bore the child out beyond the tide and buried it there, garlanded with the roses that it loved to play with, and old Egbert, who knew how the fisherman yearned for his child, wrote these words. It was said, too, that they were less what the poet thought for the fisherman than drawn from his own grief, for he had lost a child, years before, whose death and burial he never had seen."

Philip sang: —

"O wave, uprearing on the sands,
Thou hast ridden hard, hast ridden far;
Bring me no word from foreign lands,
Drop me no light from distant star:
Out of the depths of the sunless sea,
Bring back my little one to me.

"O wave that ripplest on the beach,
Thou laughest low, thou laughest light;
Bring me no mocking sea-sprite's speech,
Sing me no song of moony night:
My child lies low in the silent sea,
Bring back her tender voice to me.

"I sent her away with the roses red,
I kissed her cheek, and kissed her hand,

And she has made her curtained bed
'Neath dark sea-waves on flinty sand.
Come forth, come forth from the midnight sea,
O little child, come back to me."

"And has he then a word for every troubled heart?"

"He has words for all, for he has never shut his love up within himself, or suffered any unworthy object to draw it from him. Nevertheless, those whom men drive from them he receives, for he sees in them not that for which men thrust them forth, but that which is the beginning of heaven in them."

"The moon has risen, the night is nearly gone," said the Princess; "come with me a few steps that I may show you the beginning of this brook."

They rose from the seat, and climbing a little knoll, came to the spring from which the brook set forth on its journey; but as the water rose to the ground, it fell over a rocky steep, and was caught for a moment in a marble basin, and then, falling over its sides, slipped down a smooth stone to its channel, and so went moving onward. By the light of the moon they could see the figures which nature and art had drawn upon the marble. A clinging moss was slowly forming over it, and the grass was growing rank above it, while on the sides of the basin had been sculptured laughing Loves that formed an encircling, merry company. In the moonlight they seemed alive, dancing in speechless merriment to silent music. The two stood by the fountain, listening to the fall of the water, and then slowly returned to the rude seat by the willow.

The Princess stood looking into the water in a reverie, and then, turning to Philip, said, —

"The old man of whom you spoke — does he still live?"

"Yes, lady."

She drew her robe about her and half turning away, spoke again, —

"Master Philip, shall you paint to-morrow in the Rose-house?"

"Yes, Lady Rosella."

"And when you have finished your work you will go away?"

"There is nothing that should keep me here but your command."

"I would that I might send something to old Egbert. He would not care for the Rosella Rose? You know I despised that."

"He would despise nothing that came with love."

"To-morrow, then, I will send him the flower. Good-night."

She had spoken with her face averted, but now she turned full upon him. In the clear moonlight her eyes rested upon him with a soft, gentle look. She even smiled, as she had not smiled that night, and then turned away. He took a step as if to follow her.

"Do not come with me," she said, "I must go to the palace alone."

He watched her retreating form, till it was hidden in the shadow and he saw her no more.

## IV.

A clash of cymbals! a beating of drums! a blare of trumpets! On the roof of the palace the flags are flying, banners waving back and forth, and long pennants stream gayly out, striving to detach themselves, as it were, and fly over the palace and garden and camp, to see what wonderful sights are filling all eyes. In the camp without the gates, horses stand champing their bits and impatiently pawing as they hear the distant drum beat, and the gentlemen and attendants are busy preparing for the joyous entrance into the royal domain.

Philip, painting the Rosella Rose, heard the music and distant shouts. It was mid-morning, and his work was not yet done, but at noon he knew the procession of maidens would come, attending the Princess Rosella, to gather the wonderful Rose. So he worked diligently on, wondering meanwhile to himself how the Princess would manage to give him the rose from the bush which he was to bear to Egbert.

The Rosella Rose herself must have been aware that her hour was at hand. Slowly she unrolled her leaves, receiving the warm breath and the occasional gentle, moist shower which the Gardener, ever attendant, bestowed upon her. She was not alone, for these two were there, and yet each, intent on his occupation, were witless of the solemn movement, deep in the heart of the Rose. Was its hour really coming? It was the consummate production of nature and art; when it was gathered and placed on the bosom of the lovely Princess, the sharp pang which separated it from the plant was to be the token of an end to each. For itself, it was to linger a short hour in its place of glory, but the plant was to be burned and pass out of existence. Nevertheless, a sweet sense of future good possessed it which left far behind the momentary glory.

"You must now go," said the Gardener at last to the Painter, who was putting a final touch to his painting. "The Rosella Rose is at length to receive its glorious reward." He stood with his hands clasped behind him, holding his pruning-knife, for though in state, he could not be himself without his insignia of office. "For these many years I have watched and tended the Rose. I confess to a feeling of regret that it is now to pass away forever, but then it is to receive the highest honor, and that is much. I believe too, Philip, that I am to be knighted. Hark! they are coming."

Philip left the Rose-house, but lingered by it, in the shrubbery. The Gardener stood beside the Rose, as its faithful guardian, to abide by it to the end. The sound of music was heard, faintly and in regular cadence; light measured foot-falls sounded nearer, and then, winding with the path, came the little pageant. Maidens in sweet company bore, some plaintive music-reeds, some silken banners. They were without adornment, but their beauty shone forth, heightened by the green foliage, and by the darting hither and thither of the golden orioles that flew above their heads. In the midst moved the Princess Rosella, clad not in white as were the rest, but in a pale sea-green robe which floated from her in waving folds. She was in the midst of the procession, which parted at the door-way, leaving her to enter the little bower alone. It had been granted the Gardener as a special favor that he should sever the Rose from the bush and present it to the Princess, and accordingly he stood beside it with his knife, awaiting her coming. She entered, and bowing to the Gardener, said, —

"Wilt thou, Master Gardener, give me to wear the Rose which thou hast nourished so long and carefully?"

"Princess Rosella, most beautiful of women, I adorn thee with a new grace, the mingled gift of nature and art. Wear it on thy bosom."

"And is it mine to hold and to bestow, laying it in whatsoever hand I will?"

"Princess Rosella, who now bearest the Rosella Rose, it is thine without recall, to hold or to bestow."

The Princess left the bower, adorned with the glorious Rose. There burst forth from the lips of the maidens, receiving her again, a joyous song, and with twittering of birds and music they moved toward the palace, where the grand ceremony was to be observed, the Princess Rosella to be betrothed to the Prince Gladiolus, and to lay in his hand as token the Rosella Rose.

The Painter lingered about the Rose-house, but its glory was gone, and he, too, moved toward the palace. Something drew him away, however; some feeling which led him to turn his back on all the gorgeous pageantry and to seek again the willow and the secluded seat overhanging the brook. In the broad daylight there was a different look about the place, and Philip, remembering her word of the night before, said to himself, "Let her carry the flower herself, if she will. There was no daylight on her promise." He kept on by the brook-side, watching its course and following its little turns. He was leaving the palace and all behind, and in his heart he felt a strong desire to go back to his old home. Thither he bent his steps.

At that moment the procession of maidens had reached the palace court. Music flowed from every turret and tower, rising and falling like the waving flags which sprang into the air. From the gate on the other side advanced, at the same time, the cavalcade of Prince Gladiolus, in crimson and golden trappings, with loud, joyous blare of trumpets and resonance of horns. The court-yard was a wondrous fold of rare beauty and mighty valor. Upon a throne sat the King and Queen.

The King smiled good-naturedly, as if the ceremony would otherwise be too full of pomp, but the Queen's eye wandered restlessly over the gathering, fearful of some misplacement or calamity.

The Prince and Princess advanced to the foot of the throne, and stood face to face. For the first time Rosella looked upon Gladiolus, and saw his royal bearing and courtly grace. A herald advanced.

"Good masters all, loyal subjects of our Sovereign Lord and our Sovereign Lady, gentlemen of the court of the puissant Prince Gladiolus, hear our words. The Prince has sought the hand of the royal Princess Rosella, fairest of women, and would lay at her feet his kingdom, his crown, and his own royal person. The law of the land is just and righteous. The King commands the betrothal, and the royal Princess shall bestow upon the kneeling royal Prince a guerdon of her devoted affection, whereupon he shall rise and seal his troth with a token of his knightly honor and royal protection. The law of the land is just and righteous. Hearken to the forfeit. It is declared now, as it ever has been declared in the realm, that no princess shall receive a suitor against her will and consent; but if any noble princess be contumacious in the presence of the sovereign and court, then shall her robes of state be stripped from her, and she shall be cast forth from the presence of the noble and mighty. O King, live forever."

Loud from the mouths of trumpets and horns burst the glad music, high above the sounding drums and clash of cymbals rose the fine melody of the stringed instruments, and then, as the soft flutes breathed a blessing, the King rose from his chair of state, saying: —

"Kneel, Gladiolus; receive the guerdon."

"Rise, Prince Gladiolus, untouched by my hand."

It was the Princess Rosella who, with hands clasped before her, spoke low. There was a tumult in the crowd. "What said she?" "Does not receive him?" "Abandons all?" were the questions that passed from lips to lips; and hushed voices whispered, "See the Prince!"

Gladiolus had risen at the word, and with face aglow and eyes of fire, struck his hand upon his sword, while his gentlemen flashed their poniards in the air and cried, "Treachery! treachery!"

"Take her away! take her away!" cried the Queen, in a paroxysm of anger. "Take her away! She is no child of mine that would disgrace me thus!"

"Let her go! let her go!" said the old King, turning uneasily from one side to another. "Get her out of the way. Don't let me see her. Don't let me see her any more at all."

The court-yard was in an uproar, some declaring one thing, some another. The courtiers who had looked significantly at one another during the occasion, now said openly, that, Princess or no Princess, they had hated her from the beginning, and knew that evil would come from her in some shape. The Prince and his retinue rode angrily away, and bitter threats of open war were flung on every side. The musicians slunk away, and the banners and streamers and flags drooped heavily, as a sultry, motionless air enveloped the place.

Most angry of all was the Gardener, who exclaimed bitterly, —

"Is this the end of my years of toil and care? To be thrown away on a shrewish, low-born girl, who has laughed at me and jibed at me, morning and night. Curses on her head. May she make her bed in mire, and on the sands of the sea-shore!"

He ran to the Rose-house, and madly snatching at the cherished bush, though its thorns pierced his quivering hands, he bore it into the open air, and flung it with fury as far as his frenzied strength could impel it.

There was a gathering by the palace of some who were curious to see the expulsion of the Princess, doubting not that some ceremony would take place, not indeed so brilliant as that which had been interrupted, but even more pleasing to them.

"There she is! there she is!" at last was the cry, as the great door of the palace was opened and a figure came forward, passed the portal, and stood outside for a moment. The door closed behind her, and a pale, beggarly clad maiden, with her hands clasped over her bosom, stepped forth, descended the staircase, and moved down the garden. Rosella, for she it was, seemed heedless of the curious gathering, only watchful, apparently, that the Rose which she sheltered on her bosom, received no harm. Yet while every eye was turned upon her, none did more than whisper. No voice was raised, and the ranks divided as she passed through the midst of them. In the days of her grandeur Rosella's queenly mien awed the people, but now there was another spirit in her presence which hushed them and kept them bound by a gentle spell. None followed her, and she looked not behind but kept on, past the Rose-house, to the willow and to the bench by the brook-side. Here she sat her down for one moment, here she kneeled on the green turf, and, rising up, began to follow the windings of the stream, on, on, beyond the garden, beyond the palace park, on into green fields and through dark woods.

The day was drawing to a close, but the hot air which had weighed heavily on the earth, was now full of ominous portents. Low rumble of a gathering storm broke on the ear, and added to it was the sullen roar of the distant sea. Deep answered to deep, and sudden bursts of wind swept over the plain and hurled forward a flying figure by the banks of the brawling stream. On she sped, the wind driving her pitilessly, mocking her distress by whirling suddenly about and confronting her struggling form. On she strove, and caught again by the eddying gust, was dashed forward through bending grass. Drops from the heavy cloud above came one by one, first with a startling splash upon her face, then quicker, quicker, quicker, pelting her with a cruel glee, till she stooped beneath their thick-falling blows. Yet on she struggled toward the deep baying sea, which sounded like some mighty monster waiting for her as she was driven toward it.

And now full before her was the broad ocean, behind her still the driving storm. Where was refuge for her? what harbor from sea and storm into which she might drag her wearied body? She could not tell, and yet a dark form was before her; she lifted her poor voice and cried,—

"Father Egbert!"

Suddenly, as when in the darkness a light appears in the window, a voice answered,—

"Who calls me?"

Rosella followed the voice, herself speechless.

"Who calls me?" he asked again, and his voice was like a lantern flashing in the darkness before a wanderer.

"Who calls me? I am here."

Rosella, trembling, drew nearer to the voice, trusting in it. A strong arm reached out toward her, and found her, and drew her in, and shut the door. Rosella and the Rose were sheltered.

The morning light shone on the sea that ran lightly upon the shore. It glistened in the grass and bushes that were still hung with drops of rain. What eye that looked on the scene but saw a world of beauty, the mirror of perfection; yet what voice could speak that perfection? None indeed, though perchance there were some, who, walking then through this scene, shed from their thoughts the breath of desire which was redolent of words needing not to be spoken. From the sea, by the brook-side there walked two, old Egbert and the maiden Rosella.

"Dear daughter," said he, "it was along this path that I led your little feet on that day, years ago, when the King and Queen rode by. Can you remember this place?"

"I do not know; some faint recollection comes to me. Was there a brook near by?"

"Even here, for we are come to it," and so saying, they parted the bushes and looked into the rippling water.

"It was here," said the old man, "that I left you playing with little Philip in the brook, whilst I went back to the cottage. Bitter day that did not bring you back, but the weeping boy alone, who knew only that a man dressed in gold and scarlet bore you smiling away."

Rosella stood playing with the Rose which she held in her hand.

"Let us bury it here," said she, and stooping down by a cluster of rose-bushes, they gently opened the moist earth. Rosella took the Rose which she had borne, still flushed with beauty, and laid it softly in its bed, as if it might suffer from rude handling. They stood for a moment smiling down upon it. The morning was in them, and their hearts were opened to receive the breathing of the Rose.

The Rose, in its earthly bed, lay looking up to them, and the breathed fragrance sought them: —

"Now I am laid in my old home by the nestling of the pleasant waters, in the hearing of the mighty sea. For this was I not gathered? Dear life that is to come to me — I know not what it shall be, but it must be well; it was well even in the King's garden, though I knew not how; deep in the stirring of my heart I felt an old life that was never quenched, and now I know that there is that coming which shall keep the old good and build a greater on it."

At this moment there was a disturbance in the water; they looked and saw a dark object floating down the stream, swaying to one side and the other.

"It is a bush," said Egbert.

"It is the Rose-bush!" exclaimed Rosella,

who recognized its familiar form. It was, indeed, the Rosella Rose-bush, which, flung by the Gardener's rage, had fallen upon the brook and travelled through the night thus far, when it was arrested.

"Why not plant it here with the Rose?" said Egbert.

"Why, so we will," said the pleased girl, and she stooped down.

And now they covered the Rose at the roots of the bush, and turned away, gathering the delicate wild roses from the crowded bushes.

"Wear this now, Marina," said the old man, and he placed a rose in her bosom where once Rosella had rested.

The brook flows on into the sea, and still overhanging its waters are the bushes with their burden of flowers. Children play again in the rippling stream, sailing their tiny boats, and freighting them with the wild roses.

"Come, Rosy," says a child, "let us gather some of the strange roses."

"Why, they are not strange in our house," replies the little girl. "We have a fresh one there every day."

It was to the bushes about, that this Rose-bush with its burdens was strange. What flower, so like themselves yet with a sweet richness which they knew not, had crept in among them? The traveller, richly laden with wonderful memories, comes home, and unburdens first his older, sweeter memories; so the strange rose by the brook-side breathed not of the gorgeous life once investing it, but of the earlier days; yet still there clung to it a fragrance and a color which came not from the brook-side, from the marsh, or from the sea.

www.ingramcontent.com/pod-product-compliance
Lightning Source LLC
LaVergne TN
LVHW010216110826
845151LV00004B/1108

* 9 7 8 1 4 2 5 5 2 7 3 1 0 *